A1

and the
Beast of Chicago

Mike Casto

STEPHE,

THANKS FOR TWISTING
MY ARM, GETTING MR TO
TCA, AND CHANGING
MY LIFE.

LOVE YA, BROTHER

ISBN: 1973920298
ISBN-13: 978-1973920298

To my wife, Margaret, who is as much a hero
to me as Annie Oakley

Table of Contents

ACKNOWLEDGMENTS

I want to thank Joe R. Lansdale for his personal mentorship in so many areas and his posts on Facebook, which so often turned out to be just the kick in the pants I needed. The various bits of wisdom he has shared in person, in interviews, and on Facebook, not to mention the example he has set in his own writing, have all been of great value to me. I'm honored to call him a friend. I could write a lot more about him and his influence on me but I don't want to look like a kiss ass so I'll leave it here.

First, all thanks to my wonderful wife, Margaret Westlake. She's amazing and inspiring in so many ways. Not the least of which is her willingness to put up with me, whether I'm sequestered in a room writing or off teaching martial arts halfway around the world, she's always rooting for me. She's strong enough to do her own things and pursue her own interests while also appreciating and supporting me in mine. I'm not ashamed to say our relationship is pretty awesome and the envy of many people, even if they think we're nuts.

This story wouldn't have been possible without Harold Schechter's excellent biography of H. H. Holmes, *Depraved*. Thank you, Mr. Schechter, for the time and effort you spent writing such an entertaining and informational resource for my own research.

Similarly, I owe a sizable measure of gratitude to Larry McMurtry's *The Colonel and Little Missie,* which helped me develop a feel for the relationship between Buffalo Bill and Annie Oakley.

I used many other resources. Some, such as Buffalo Bill's biography and Holmes's memoirs, I found at Project Gutenberg (http://www.gutenberg.org).

Thanks to Gypsy Shadow Publishing for picking up the eBook version of this story. Working with Denise and Charlotte was a pleasure.

CHAPTER ONE

Sunday, April 30, 1893

Annie and Cody took in the view from an observation deck overlooking the buildings of the White City, which stood in stark contrast to the grimy city of Chicago outside the fairgrounds. The pearly veneers of the neoclassical architecture gleamed in the afternoon sun, pristine and virginal, in opposition to the sooty urban blight. Like a bride, resplendent in her white gown, standing in the middle of a muddy street, her hem held at the perfect height to keep it above the muck while still remaining modest.

Annie said, "It's amazing."

Colonel William F. "Buffalo Bill" Cody looked down at the petite woman walking next to him. Her long sleeved light brown dress complimented her dark brown eyes and long brown hair exquisitely. Cody knew, like most of her clothes, she'd made the dress with her own hands.

He'd always considered her an attractive woman, but thought of her more as a little sister or a niece than with any romantic interest. What intrigued and impressed him most, though, lay in her ability to outshoot him, or most anyone else in the world for that matter.

"I concur, Annie. This is a fascinating sight to behold."

The World's Fair, dubbed the World Columbian Exposition to note the 400th anniversary of Columbus' arrival in the New World, would open the next morning. Cody's Wild West show, denied a formal slot in the Expo, had rented a parcel of land three blocks south of the Midway Plaisance and set up shop. The show's performers and promoters had spent the past couple of weeks preparing feverishly to perform two shows daily throughout the next six months of the Expo.

At Bill's request, and with some fancy talking, Cody's partner, Nate, persuaded the reluctant fair administrators to grant Cody a sneak peek at the fairgrounds before the opening. He and Annie had strolled through the grounds, admiring the grandeur.

Now, from their vantage atop the Manufactures and Liberal Arts building, the Court of Honor dominated the scene before them. Below, the Statue of the Republic overlooked the Grand Basin, which symbolized the voyage Columbus took to the New World. Waterways branched off the large pool and ran between the buildings of the Court. Cody could just make out a line of Venetian gondolas bobbing at the piers around the buildings, waiting for the throngs of fairgoers that would descend upon them soon.

Cody thought, *Seeing the White City from a gondola cruising slowly along the waterways between the buildings would be incredible. Louisa would love this*. Unfortunately, his wife wasn't with him here in the White City. Nevertheless, he planned to find time for one of those cruises once the show got under way. His mind wandered to thoughts of his children. Arta, 27, still lived at home, and helped Louisa take care of the house and the precocious little ten year old Irma. *Maybe I shall write to Louisa. See if she and the girls can come visit. They should see this ephemeral spectacle. God knows it won't last.*

Reluctantly, he dragged his mind back to the here and now. A brisk nip rode the air, but the sun shone brightly, and cut the chill just enough to make it pleasant. A few clouds lingered in the blue sky. Their shadows danced like specters on the surfaces of the white buildings as they glided overhead.

"You propose to shoot a playing card edge-on from ninety feet, cutting it in half, then shoot the falling half at least three more times before it hits the ground?"

"That, indeed, is what I propose. I've been practicing, and I can do it consistently. It'll be a crowd pleaser."

His bushy mustache lifted as he smiled. "I reckon it will. I know I shall be impressed. Let us adjourn to our shooting range and you can, once again, amaze me while I work out some patter for the showmanship side of things."

As usual, Annie fluttered her eyelashes and flashed a shy little smile at the compliment. The genuine sincerity of this mannerism, and others like it, captivated Cody. Annie's magnificent stage presence stemmed from her honesty, not her acting. This same trait had swept Annie's rough and tumble husband, Frank, off his feet, and had gained her the adoration of millions of fans all over the world.

Cody felt honored she'd chosen to work in his show and had stayed for so long. The previous year, she and Frank had left the show for a time and toured on their own in Europe, all because of Lillian Smith. His own blindness to Annie's disfavor of Lillian rankled him still.

I really should have fired Lillian at the first signs of jealousy from Annie. Lillian was a fine shot, and her youth intrigued the crowds for a time. But Annie ... well, she's Little Sure Shot.

Few people could work an audience as adroitly as Annie. Fewer still could shoot half as well. Not a particularly religious man, Cody agreed with old Sitting Bull that the Great Spirit had gifted Annie with supernatural shooting prowess.

Touching her temple lightly, Annie grimaced. "I've been troubled by headaches quite a bit recently. I saw a pharmacy not far from the Midway. Give me an hour or so. I need to purchase some headache powder. Then I'll retrieve a long gun and ammunition from my tent and meet you in the field."

CHAPTER TWO

As the door opened, it tapped a small bell mounted above it. The pharmacist looked up from where he worked at a bench behind the counter at the back of the room. "I'll be with you in a moment, miss. This particular mixture requires a fair bit of concentration to get it right."

Annie smiled. "Take your time. I'm in no rush." She regarded him as he worked, a man of average height, a bit on the stocky side, with a thick mustache and thinning brown hair. In most ways he was quite unremarkable, except for his hands. They moved among the chemicals, selecting a pinch of this and pouring a dash of that, stirring and mixing. Annie stood, head and body turned sideways to the man, but watching with her peripheral vision in fascination. His hands seemed to have a mind of their own. It was like watching a master magician at work, impossible to follow his exact motions from moment to moment. After a few minutes, he paused. Nodding to himself, he set the mixture aside and stepped over to the counter.

His eyes roamed over her, assessing her in the same way he'd measured ingredients for the mixture. She looked to be in her late twenties or early thirties. A little older than the women who normally caught his attention, but she was a very attractive woman nonetheless. *She looks familiar. Where have I seen her before?* After a moment, he had it.

"Hello, sir. I find myself in need of some headache powder."

"Oh, dear. A headache in your line of work could be very dangerous indeed."

Annie smiled. "You recognize me?" She looked straight into his eyes. Peering from beneath his bushy eyebrows, they reminded her of a cat's eyes--somehow predatory and disinterested at the same time.

His thumbs hooked into the waist pockets of his dark brown vest. "How could I not, Miss Oakley. Your celebrity precedes you. Your face is well known to anyone who follows current affairs. I am Dr. Henry Holmes, and I'm honored to make your acquaintance." He extended a hand across the counter. She extended her hand, and he neatly raised it to his lips, kissing her knuckle lightly.

She smiled politely, gently disengaging from his grip.

"Give me a moment to get your headache powder." He ducked through a curtain at the back of the room. Annie adjusted her hat and pressed her thumbs against her throbbing temples. She leaned against the wooden counter top and surveyed the store's wares through squinting eyes.

The small shop appeared well stocked. A long set of freestanding shelves ran down the middle of the room, and more shelves lined the walls, stocked neatly with various tonics, tinctures, colognes, perfumes, and other items common to pharmacies. The place smelled mostly of disinfectant and wood polish, with an odd chemical odor, probably related to the mixture he'd just prepared. A stack of flyers, advertising rooms for rent in *The World's Fair Hotel*, lay on the sturdy, hardwood counter, and caught Annie's attention.

Holmes returned from the back room and set a box on the counter. "Arabian Headache Powder. The finest available today. I just received it in this morning's shipment and haven't had time to put it on the shelves yet. It should quell your headaches rapidly and thoroughly."

Annie sighed, already imagining the relief. "Wonderful. How much do I owe you for this box?"

Holmes waved dismissively. "My dear, your show will take place barely two miles from my front door. I have no doubt your presence so near to my establishment will have a profound effect on my business in the coming months. Consider this box my payment to you for the increase in my sales. All I ask in return is that you recommend my shop to anyone you encounter who needs anything I might provide."

Picking up one of the flyers, he said, "As to what I might provide, this pharmacy is but one of my endeavors. I own this entire building. It covers an entire city block, and many in the neighborhood refer to it as *The Castle* because of the rounded turret-like appearance at the corners. I offer rooms for rent on the second floor. They aren't extravagant, but they're comfortable and reasonably priced. They're especially well-suited to women, since they offer the ultimate in privacy and security. If you'd like, I can give you a special rate on my best room during your stay in our fair city."

Annie found the comment about privacy and security a bit much, but she couldn't really fault him. She knew enough about show business and marketing to recognize an effort to appeal to the audience.

She smiled again, ignoring the pain of her headache. "Thank you, sir, but I'll be quite happy in my tent. As far as my security, the troop watches out for its own and, failing that, my guns and my husband should prove more than adequate."

Holmes twitched. "I had no idea you were married."

"We don't advertise it. My husband is also my press agent, and he believes it makes me seem more approachable if people don't know. I assure you, though, I am quite happily married."

"I'm sorry, ma'am. I meant no disrespect."

"None taken, sir. I just wanted to lay my cards on the table, so to speak, to avoid any misunderstandings. I appreciate the offer."

Picking up the tin of medicine, she continued. "And the powder. I will certainly recommend your store and your rooms to anyone I encounter who may benefit from your services. Thank you." Still holding the flyer for the hotel, she gave him a parting curtsy, turned, and walked out of the store.

Holmes stroked his mustache and watched her exit the store. He kept watching through the front window as she turned right and pulled a bicycle away from where she had leaned against the wall next to the window. Putting the flyer and tin of powder in a small basket on the front of the bike, she stepped over the low cross bar, and pedaled east toward the fair grounds.

CHAPTER THREE

Monday, May 8, 1893

A light shower had fallen the night before, not enough to make the ground muddy, but the light breeze still carried the faint scent of rain.

Ninety feet away, the ace of spades sat mounted in a vice with the edge facing Annie. She squeezed the trigger slowly. The shot carved the top half of the card from the bottom and sent it spiraling upward momentarily.

All of her ammunition, custom made for the show, fired a fine mist of shot instead of solid bullets. On learning this, some people thought it made the trick shots easier, a type of cheat. But, really, within its effective range, the shot didn't spread much more than the size of a bullet anyway, so it didn't make it any easier to hit targets. It did, however, minimize the chance of an accident. If, by some freak chance, some of the pellets of shot did reach the audience, they could do no more damage than a tiny rock thrown by the hoof of one of the horses in the show. Even within the effective range of the round, the shot would do far less damage than a bullet. It was more than adequate, though, to cut cards, burst glass bulbs, and send coins spinning.

As the card fluttered back toward the ground, Annie smoothly worked the lever action and fired again. And again. She fired four times before the card finally settled on the dewy grass. With each echoing report from her Marlin, the card hopped a little in the air. She lowered the gun from her shoulder. Nearly 20,000 people filled the grandstand to see the amazing prowess of the world's best trick shot artist. They had gasped and applauded with each report of Annie's rifle. Now they waited, holding their collective breath, while Frank ran over, pressing his bowler hat firmly down on his head. He knelt to pick up the tattered card from the ground.

By this point, the end of her first show of the day, Annie had found her stride, and knew all four shots had found their mark as the card fell. Nonetheless, she put on a good show for the crowd. Resting the butt of her gun on the ground, she clasped her hands around the barrel as if anxiously awaiting the verdict. The light breeze rustled her buckskin skirt and the fringes on her sleeves. The wide brim of her Stetson shielded her eyes from the sun overhead.

Frank, quite the showman himself, picked up the card and examined it carefully, letting the tension build. After a long thirty seconds or so, he let out a whoop and pumped his fist in the air as he announced there were four holes in it. The audience exploded with applause and excited yells. Annie curtsied as she had learned in Europe, and the audience erupted even louder. They rose to give her a standing ovation. She clapped cheerfully along with the crowd, smiling and blowing kisses their way. Cody came striding across the field, his long legs carrying him quickly from his seat to stand beside Annie.

His height, accentuated by the cut of his white buckskins and his commanding presence, quieted the crowd. His rich baritone voice carried across the space and reached the farthest parts of the stands with no apparent effort. "What an amazing display of marksmanship! Or should I say marks-*woman*-ship? Ladies and gentlemen, you've just seen Miss Annie Oakley, the belle of sharpshooters, in action. She will do another show at six o'clock. Make sure you tell your friends about it, and I'm sure we'll see some of you again. It is always a treat to watch Miss Oakley in action.

"We are going to take a short break and, when we return, we'll bring out the Congress of Rough Riders of the World, and treat you to some incredible horsemanship with some of the best riders the world has ever seen. During the break, make sure to visit the merchandise stalls and pick up your souvenirs. You will also find many of our performers, including the inimitable Annie Oakley, Little Sure Shot herself, signing autographs."

Even as she felt a twinge of grief, Annie smiled at the nickname given to her by Sitting Bull during his tenure with the company. The two grew very close during their relatively short acquaintance a few years before. News of his death had left her heart broken, and thinking of him still brought a twinge of pain. To top things off, she had learned something upsetting about the fair a few days before.

One of the attractions on the Midway was the actual cabin where her old friend had been murdered. She had gone to the fair managers a week before and asked permission to visit the cabin after hours. In darkness, she sat in the place for a long time, replaying fond memories of the kindly old Sioux holy man who'd been so kind to her, and who had ritualistically adopted her as a daughter. The bittersweet memories poured over her.

The news of Sitting Bull's murder by Indian Police had infuriated Annie. *If he'd been a white man, someone would have hung.* So many whites thought of the Indians as inferior. Annie had dealt with many Indians while working for the Wild West and many, many white folks all over America and in Europe. One thing was clear to her after all those years. People were people. The color of their skin didn't matter so much. Some were good and some were rotten. The whole idea of racial superiority sickened her.

Annie sat at the table signing autographs. Her Marlin .22 lever action custom smoothbore, the same gun she had used to shoot the card in the last show, lay unloaded on the table next to her. It had taken her a while to get accustomed to popularity and signing autographs. Even longer for her to realize people wanted to see and touch the firearms she used in her shows. When signing autographs, she used a Wirt fountain pen given to her by Cody when she and Frank returned to the show following their hiatus. It wrote smoothly and fit comfortably in her small grip.

A petite feminine hand placed a handbill for the show, featuring a portrait of Annie, on the table. Annie looked up to see a young woman, probably in her early twenties, wearing a dark blue dress with a heavy shawl and a straw boater hat with a wide dark blue band. Annie smiled. "Would you like a personal message? Or just a signature?"

The younger woman blushed and quietly said something. Annie couldn't quite make it out. "Pardon me? There's a lot of background noise. Could you speak up, please?"

The woman leaned forward and said in a clearer voice, "Please address it to Sophia."

Annie, who always tried to make autographs feel personal, thought for a moment, then wrote, "To Sophia, I love your hat. Annie Oakley." She slid the paper back to the young lady.

Sophia read it. Her hand reached up to her hat, her eyes widened, and she beamed. "I really am one of your biggest fans, Miss Oakley. Thanks ever so much!"

"You are very welcome, Sophia. Where are you from? Your accent sounds midwestern."

"A town called Trotwood. Near Dayton, Ohio."

It was Annie's turn to beam. "Why, that's just down the road from where I grew up."

"Yes, ma'am."

"Pshaw! No need to ma'am me, Sophia. Call me Annie. You've come a long way to this event. Has it been worth the trip?"

Sophia blushed. "Yes, ma--Annie. I came just to see you. I've followed your career as well as I can. When I read in the newspaper you were going to be performing here, I simply had to come see you in person. You're my idol, Annie."

"Really? Why me? I'm just a simple farm girl from Ohio. God gave me a knack for shooting, but many people have much better talents, things much more helpful to the world."

"It's not about your shooting, impressive as it is. It's because you really are a simple farm girl from Ohio. Same as me. But you've become a celebrity. You've carved out a place in the world for yourself, and you're a peer to some of the biggest names in the world. I doubt I'll ever achieve anything so grand, but knowing you did it inspires me to think I might do something grand myself."

Annie thought for a moment. "My advice, Sophia, is to aim for a high mark. I expect you'll hit it. Not on the first shot, nor the second. Maybe not the third. But keep on aiming and keep on shooting, and practice will make you perfect. Eventually you'll hit it every time. Then raise your sights and aim even higher."

"I reckon those are words to live by. I'm more honored than you can know to have met you and had this chance to talk to you. Thank you."

Sophia blushed and turned to walk away.

"Wait! Sophia, would you like to have dinner with me? I would dearly love to reminisce about home."

Sophia stopped and turned back around. The look on her face was a mixture of surprise, happiness, and disbelief. For a second, Annie thought the young woman might faint, but she regained her composure quickly. "Of course!"

Annie smiled. "I'll be here for the next twenty minutes or so. After Colonel Cody calls for the next show to start, you come back to this table, and I'll meet you here." Sophia seemed to glow with excitement.

"I will! Oh, I will!"

Sophia returned to the table as Annie was signing her last autograph for the session. The last person in line was a young man, about 15 years old, with dark brown hair, high cheekbones, and a broad, infectious smile. He laid a small notebook on the table, and Annie asked, "To whom should I sign this?"

"Will Rogers, ma'am. It's a right pleasure to meet you, ma'am."

Annie wished the young man well, and as he walked away, she placed her pen carefully in its cushioned case, closed it, and picked up her Marlin. She turned to Sophia. "I must return these items to my tent. Then we can find a place to eat and talk." .

The entrance to Annie's tent was ten feet wide with a wooden porch built out from it. A sign over the entrance read, "Annie Oakley." Annie pulled back one of the flaps and tied it open. The spacious interior surprised Sophia. A bed occupied the left wall. A small writing desk, with papers neatly stacked on it, sat against the right wall. Annie's bicycle leaned against the front wall. A couple of rocking chairs nestled in the back corners, and a chifforobe stood against the back wall with a rack of long guns next to it. Several photos and portraits leaned against the remaining open spaces of the tent walls. Some depicted Annie, either posed, or in action with her firearms. Others portrayed a man whom Sophia recognized as Frank Butler, Annie's sharpshooter husband.

Annie set down her things. She noticed the handbill she had signed still rolled into a tube in Sophia's hand. "Maybe we should visit your lodgings first, so you can put your souvenir safely with your belongings."

Sophia blushed lightly. "After train fare and the price of admission to the Wild West show I'm afraid I don't have enough money to afford worthwhile lodgings. I thought I might find a cheap boarding house but I've had no such luck."

"Oh dear! Where will you sleep?"

"Last night, the hostler at the stables down the way let me sleep in one of his unused stalls. I left my luggage, what little there is, in a locker at the train station."

"No, no. We can't have you sleeping in a horse stall."

"Really, Annie, I grew up on a farm. I've spent a lot of time in stables and horse stalls."

Annie remembered her conversation with the pharmacist the week before. "Hold on a moment." She turned and rummaged through some papers on the writing desk. "Ah!" She pulled a sheet of paper from the stack and handed it to Sophia.

Large, bold type letters at the top of the flyer read, "Welcome to the World's Fair Hotel!" Below the headline, a picture of a large three story brick building with rounded turret-like structures at the corners and a lot of windows dominated a third of the page. The text of the flyer read, "Welcome to Chicago, the world-renowned Windy City! I, Dr. H. H. Holmes, welcome you to the World's Fair Hotel. The rooms are comfortable, private, and well-appointed at a very reasonable price.

"If you're in town for the World's Columbian Exposition then you're in luck! The building is less than two miles from the Midway. It's a pleasant walk, or you can catch a street car. We also have bicycles for rent.

"We're located at the south corner of 63rd and South Wallace Street. During business hours you'll find me working in my pharmacy on the ground floor. After business hours simply pull the bell cord hanging by the door to the pharmacy and I will come down to meet you from my apartment over the store. I look forward to helping you make your visit to Chicago one to remember."

Sophia read the flyer and asked, "Do you know how much he charges for a room?"

Annie shrugged. "He offered me a special rate when I talked to him last week. I'm sure I can convince him to extend the same rate to you. In fact, I would be happy to pay the rent myself. I hate to think of a fellow Buckeye sleeping in a stable when I can help her get a comfortable room."

"Oh no, I don't want to impose on your good nature, nor burden you with unnecessary expense. If the room is affordable, then I will rent it. If not, then I will seek other lodgings. Something I can afford."

"I'll tell you what. If you can't afford a room at Holmes's hotel then, at least, I can offer you a pallet here in my tent. It will certainly be better than a stable."

"Sharing a tent with you would be like a dream come true, but I don't want to impose."

"You're not imposing. I insist. Let's go talk to Dr. Holmes and hear his offer."

CHAPTER FOUR

Annie opened the door to the pharmacy and saw Holmes sitting behind a desk at the back of the room, writing in a large ledger. He looked up, and, seeing her, stood. He tucked his pencil behind his ear and rushed around the counter. "Miss Oakley! So good to see you again. Do you need more headache powder?"

"No, Dr. Holmes. The Arabian powder worked wonders, and I still have plenty of it. No, I've just learned this young woman is in need of lodging while in Chicago. You previously offered me a special rate for one of your rooms, and I wondered if you might extend the same rate to her."

Holmes looked at Sophia. "Of course! A friend of Annie Oakley is a friend of mine. I do have a room available. How long are you going to be in Chicago?"

"While I would love to stay longer, I fear I must return home in a couple of weeks. My train leaves Chicago early on the 24th."

"I do have weekly rates. Normally I rent for five dollars per week but I'll offer you a special rate of three dollars."

Pulling a small notebook from his vest pocket, he flipped quickly to a blank page. His pencil flew across it, jotting figures as he mumbled in a low whisper. The only words Annie could make out were tax and prorate.

"If you took residency tonight and departed the morning of the 24th your total would come to $7.50."

Annie didn't think Sophia could have looked any more surprised if a piano had materialized behind Dr. Holmes complete with a dog playing Battle Hymn of the Republic.

"I'm sorry to have troubled you, sir, but the price is considerably beyond my current means."

"I'm very sorry." Holmes looked genuinely distraught.

Annie said, "How much can you afford, Sophia?"

Sophia hesitated, blushing with embarrassment. "Not enough."

"I can pay the difference."

"No. I thank you for your offer. Thank you both for your consideration, but I will not accept charity." She began to turn away.

"Wait a moment," Holmes said.

Sophia stopped and turned to look at Holmes, who had cocked his head to the right, hand stroking his thick mustache. "Do you have any special skills? Are you good with numbers, for instance?"

"Not really. I can read, and I love books, but I have never had much need for math."

"You can read. Can you also write?"

"Yes." A hopeful note crept into her voice. She didn't know what Holmes had in mind, but his tone had piqued her curiosity.

"I had an assistant who stocked shelves for me, but she took a fancy to a traveling salesman and ran off with him. I have been meaning to hang a help wanted sign and take out an ad in the Tribune, but I have yet to do either. A foolish part of me hopes she will return. She was a good assistant.

"I know your employment would be temporary, but I could pay you five dollars per week. You could afford your room and you would come out ahead in the long run. Who knows, maybe you'll decide you like it enough to remain."

After a barely noticeable hesitation, Sophia clapped her hands and leaped forward to embrace a very surprised Holmes. Sophia stepped quickly back and clasped her hands in front of her, barely maintaining her composure. "Thank you, sir! I can't tell you how much this means to me."

Holmes chuckled. "Based on your reaction, I think I can make a reasonably accurate guess."

CHAPTER FIVE

Tuesday, May 16, 1893

Annie and Sophia had become fast friends in the short time since they'd met and had established a standing dinner date. Sometimes Frank or Cody joined them but, most nights, it the two women ate alone. They had found an Italian restaurant they adored at the west end of the Midway. After a few visits to Cucina di Mamma, the restaurant staff asked Annie for her permission to advertise her patronage.

Her celebrity brought many people into the restaurant, all hoping to catch a glimpse of the famous woman or get a chance to meet her. The owner, Mamma Aquila herself, often stopped by to talk to them as they ate their desserts. She seemed very fond of the younger women, and called them her *nipotinas*, Italian for niece.

Annie gladly entertained fans who stopped by the table, as did Frank and Cody during their visits. At first, Sophia's proximity to the center of attention overwhelmed her, but she gradually grew accustomed to it.

This particular night, though, Annie felt the urge for some privacy, so they sat in one of the booths at the back of the room with privacy curtains.

After they settled into the booth, Annie noticed Sophia's mischievous smile.

"What is it, Sophia?" Annie asked.

"Mr. Jameson gave me a box of imported chocolates. All the way from Switzerland." Sophia pulled a small box from her pocket and set it on the table between them. Several chocolates fit snuggly inside. Sophia and Mr. Jameson, the owner of the candy shop, shared a mutual passion for board games, especially *Round the World with Nellie Bly*, and had grown rather close.

They talked as they nibbled their way through the delicious chocolates. Annie asked Sophia, "So, how are things at the pharmacy?"

"Oh, very well. I enjoy the work a lot. Holmes is a pleasure to work with, and he's a very charming man. He is rather flirtatious, but never improper. I can't say the same for his friend Mr. Pietzel."

"Oh?"

"Yes. Benjamin Pietzel. Apparently, he was the foreman who oversaw the building of 'The Castle.' He's a very rough mannered man. He reminds me of an itinerant farm hand my father hired when I was about thirteen. Turned out, he only took the job on our farm as an excuse to be near town so he could plan a bank robbery.

"I don't know what Dr. Holmes sees in Pietzel, but they seem fast friends. When Pietzel visits, the two of them usually retreat to Dr. Holmes's apartment to speak in private. Pietzel hasn't done anything completely out of line toward me, but he has made some very lewd comments about women within my hearing, and I don't like him very much."

"Listen to your instincts, Sophia. Some people in this world are not people. They're wolves. Predators who only pretend to be human. They can be very dangerous. Promise me you'll never allow yourself to be alone with this Pietzel."

"I promise, Annie."

They continued eating, and their conversation turned toward lighter subjects. Sophia said, "A few months ago I was working as a seamstress in Dayton. Saving money for my trip here, in fact. One day, on my way to work, my bicycle chain broke. I had to walk the bicycle nearly a mile and was late to work. I was only thirty minutes late, but the shop owner docked me half a day's pay. Since I was only getting paid for half a day I decided to only work half a day."

Annie laughed quietly. "You surprise me, Sophia. You seem like such a quiet, reserved young lady who would never rock the boat. But then you do something or, in this case, tell me something you've done, and I'm reminded how strong and capable you really are. Few women I know would have been so bold. They would have been upset, but would have worked through the whole day."

Sophia blushed and shook her head.

Annie continued, "I mean it. Few women, of any age, would have done what you did to get here. You worked and saved your money for months. Then you, a single woman, traveling alone, boarded a train and came to Chicago to follow a dream. Your actions exhibit the very soul of bravery, and I admire you for it."

Sophia laughed quietly, bemused. "Look at you! You were only fifteen when you entered a shooting contest against a well-established marksman. You not only beat him, but wound up marrying him and earning top billing in your shows. You went on to become one of the most famous sharpshooters in the world. Now, he's your assistant and press manager and rarely performs himself. You were fifteen! The soul of bravery indeed. What I did pales in comparison."

Annie shook her head. "Not at all. I was playing to my strengths. I knew I was good at shooting. Always have been. I knew I could beat him. My actions didn't require any special bravery."

Sophia sat for a moment, a bit taken aback by this perspective. She'd never considered her own actions to be significant or special. She took a moment to gather her thoughts then, in a teasing tone, said, "I'm afraid you've derailed the story I was telling."

Annie laughed out loud and, reaching across the table, patted Sophia's arm affectionately. "I am terribly sorry, dear. Please continue."
"Where was I?"

"You left work early."

"Right. I left work early and took my bicycle to a repair shop called Wright Cycle Exchange. It had recently opened near the sewing shop. The owners were fascinating. They were brothers. Orville and Wilbur were their names. While they repaired my bicycle, they told me about their plans to build a flying machine."

Annie's eyes went wide with surprise. "A flying machine! Surely it was a joke of some sort? I heard some preposterous and funny stories in Europe about people who had tried such things. They all failed, often spectacularly. I have heard of many successful gliders, and there have been some promising dirigible efforts, but a true flying machine? According to many people more educated than I, it is simply not possible. It defies the laws of nature."

Sophia laughed. "I thought so too, but they spoke very passionately about it. I doubt it will ever be more than a fantastic dream, but their excitement about the topic was rather infectious, I must say. When I get back to Dayton, I will stop by their shop again and ask about their progress. Then I'll write to you with an update."

Annie laughed. "I would enjoy reading your letters a great deal. Speaking of Dayton, will you go back to the seamstress job? Or do have something else in mind?"

"I doubt I'll go back to being a seamstress. As I said, I was just saving money for this trip and, since I quit to come here, I doubt they would trust me if I went back. I have enjoyed working in the pharmacy here. Maybe I will find similar work there."

She paused a moment and an excited expression bloomed on her face.

"I haven't told you yet! You know the jeweler next door to the pharmacy?"

With a bob of her had, Annie indicated she did.

"Well, I found the most adorable set of earrings for sale there. Normally they would be well outside my price range, but there is a minor flaw, not even noticeable to the naked eye, in one of the stones, so they were marked down considerably. The jeweler set them aside for me, and I've been paying him each week from my earnings. I plan to give the earrings to my mother as a gift upon returning home."

"What a great idea. I'm sure she'll love them."

"I'll pick them up on my last day in Chicago so I'm less likely to lose them in my luggage or forget them somewhere."

They continued chatting through their meal, making plans for Saturday to attend the World's Congress of Representative Women at the fair, and hear Susan B. Anthony, among others, speak about Women's

Suffrage. Their friendship grew yet stronger as they discovered more and more common interests.

CHAPTER SIX

Monday, May 22, 1893

Sitting at their usual table, Annie said, "Sophia, I must tell you, you've made the past couple of weeks thoroughly enjoyable. I've developed a very sisterly fondness for you, and I value your friendship highly. Our dinners together have been great, and the day we spent seeing the sights of the fair, hearing Miss Anthony talk, was one I'll always cherish. I know you leave on Wednesday morning, and I have a favor to ask."

"Of course, Annie. I feel very sisterly toward you, too. I even wrote as much in a letter to my mother. I'll grant any favor I can."

"Tomorrow, after work, please bring your luggage to my tent. We'll spend the night talking like schoolgirls, and I'll escort you to the train station on Wednesday morning to see you off."

Sophia, wearing a smile that threatened to touch her ears, reached across the table and clasped Annie's hand as a tear slid down her cheek. "Of course, Annie.

Sounds delightful. I'd considered staying longer, and I wrote to my mother about it. In her response, she informed me of my younger brother's impending nuptials. It seems Joseph has finally worked up the gumption to ask his sweetheart, Sandra, to marry him. The wedding is scheduled for next month, so I must return home to help with the planning and, of course, to be there for the event itself.

"I want to stay in touch, though. Please write to me any time. Just send mail to Sophia Russler, General Delivery, Trotwood, Ohio."

"I definitely will, Sophia. You can send mail to me, care of the Wild West show, and it will eventually catch up with me. But I'll also make sure to write to you any time I'm more settled, like now, and give you a more specific address. Of course, we'll be here until early November and I'd love to hear from you any time you want to write."

Inhaling deeply, Sophia said, "So ... tomorrow evening, I'll bid farewell to Dr. Holmes, bring my luggage to your tent, and meet you for dinner after your six o'clock show as usual."

Annie considered a moment, then said, "I'll make sure folks around my tent know to expect you so they don't think you're a sneak thief."

Sophia laughed. "Oh, I would be so embarrassed."

CHAPTER SEVEN

Tuesday, May 23, 1893

In the morning, Sophia woke early, walked through the strange corridors of The Castle leading to the stairs, and down toward the pharmacy. Outside, a steady, gentle rain fell from the overcast sky. The sounds of the rain as it flowed down the gutters and drains running along the outside corners of the building had an almost hypnotic quality. The variously sized drainage tubes resonated like musical notes through the walls of the building. Those notes, like a lullaby, had helped her sleep the night before, although she twice awoke to noises that, through some strange trick of acoustics, had sounded like muffled screams.

Small rivulets formed lightning shaped patterns on the storefront windows. As usual, Dr. Holmes had woken before her. Only the top of his head poked above the counter as he unpacked the previous night's delivery from a box on the floor. At the sound of her footsteps, he lifted his head to peer over the counter. "Good morning,

Sophia. See the tray on the counter there with the stoppered bottles? I filled and labeled those last night. Can you sort them into their proper places on the shelves?"

"Of course, Dr. Holmes." She picked up the tray and began working.

"You leave tomorrow morning, correct?"

"Actually, I have plans to meet with Annie after work and stay with her at the Wild West show tonight. She's going to escort me to the train station tomorrow morning."

"Splendid." His voice carried an odd, distracted note.

"Is something wrong, Doctor?"

"Uhh. No. Nothing's wrong. I just remembered something. Last week, you mentioned our supply of tweezers had run low. I forgot to order new ones, and the possibility of running out of such a common item has put me in a somewhat sour mood. Something just occurred to me, though. A few months ago, I accidentally ordered more tweezers than I needed at the time, so I placed them in storage."

"I haven't noticed any boxes labeled tweezers in the back stock room."

"No, I put them in the extra storage upstairs."

"Extra storage? I didn't know there was any other storage."

A strange expression passed over Holmes's face, there and gone in the blink of an eye. It seemed as if another face had tried to emerge, as if a mask of some sort had slipped for a moment. Sophia felt a twang of unease, but it disappeared as quickly as Holmes's expression. She dismissed it as a figment of her imagination.

Holmes said, "Yes. I accommodate some long-term tenants in a couple of the rooms on the second floor, along with the short-term rooms, like the one you're renting. I use the rest of the second floor for storage. Mostly, I pack away large items up there, but there's also a room for seasonal storage, and one for miscellaneous long-term storage. I use it mostly for things like the box of tweezers, non-perishable items for which I have no immediate use."

"Would you like me to go get the box of tweezers?"

"No, no. It's a mess up there, and it would take some time to sort through everything to find the proper box. I'm not nearly as organized as you are, my dear."

"Nonsense, Doctor. Just tell me which room to search, and I'll go find the box. You have plenty of other work to do. You don't have time to go searching for a box of tweezers."

"Well. I can certainly recognize a valid argument when I hear one. I must warn you, though. It is rather dusty and very dark. Direct sunlight could harm some of the items I might store in the room, so the windows are covered.

"Come. I'll show you to the room and leave you to find the box on your own while I come back down to continue preparing for the day's business."

Holmes led the way up the stairs to the second floor. The stairway ended in a hallway, and directly in front of them lay the door to Holmes's apartment. She hadn't been in his apartment but, based on things he'd said, she had the impression it was large with many rooms.

The hall continued to the left and wound around through several open areas designed as sitting lounges for the tenants. The lodging rooms extended down the hall, just past the lounge areas. Holmes led Sophia through them and past the door to her own room.

She heard Mr. Hanson snoring from his room. The British expatriate worked nights at the train station. She sometimes saw him in the morning as he arrived home from work. She loved his accent and wished they could have talked more.

Just past the lodging rooms, they turned a corner and came to a door. Holmes unlocked it and stepped through. Sophia followed him into darkness. He paused, took a lamp from a table by the wall, and lit its wick. After replacing the glass chimney, he picked up a candle from a box sitting on the table. His smile flashed in the yellow lamplight before he turned and continued down the shadowy hallway.

The passageways in this section meandered with all sorts of turns and odd junctions. Within moments, Sophia had completely lost her bearings. "Doctor, I don't know if I'll be able to find my way back down."

"Don't worry, my dear. If you're not back downstairs in half an hour or so, then I'll come retrieve you. I designed this section, and I'm afraid it didn't live up to my expectations. I should have listened to Mr. Pietzel's counsel. He has much more experience in such matters than I do, but I vetoed his suggestions and wound up with this cumbersome collection of halls and rooms. Even I sometimes get turned around. I keep it locked so people don't accidentally get lost back here."

Finally, they rounded one last corner, and Holmes stopped in front of another door. He grasped the large ring of keys that always hung from his belt, and fumbled for the right one. "Ah ha." With a quick slide and twist of the wrist, he unlocked the door and pushed it open. From where they stood, Sophia could only see a foot or so into the room in the dim, fluttering light from the lamp's flame.

"This is the room I use for miscellaneous storage. I think I put the box of tweezers on a shelf at the far side of the room. I'll leave you to your search now, while I go finish opening the store. If you need any help, don't hesitate to ring. Take the lamp. I will use the candle to light my way back downstairs."

"Okay, Dr. Holmes." A small tremor in her voice surprised her. She hadn't been afraid of the dark in years, but for some reason she felt a chill of fear shudder through her. Her mom would have said, "A duck just walked on your grave."

With a little shrug, she took the lamp and stepped into the room. As the lamp illuminated the farthest regions of the space, it became obvious there were no shelves. Behind her, the door closed with a solid thud.

"Dr. Holmes?"

Rushing back to the door, she grabbed for the doorknob, only to be greeted by a sheer metal panel. "Dr. Holmes! What are you doing?" The palm of her hand slapped hard against the metal. Again and again. It dawned on her slowly. The sound of her pounding possessed a strange, muted timbre. "Dr. Holmes!" Her voice, reflecting off the metal door and back to her own ears, held the same odd, flattened tonality. Fear surged through her.

"Miss Russler." The voice came from high up on the wall by the door. Holding the lamp up, she could just make out a small grill near the ceiling. "Miss Russler, I do apologize for this. I had planned to do this tonight after you returned from dinner. It would have been a much more pleasant and relaxed situation.

"Then you spoiled those plans, and I had to improvise. I do apologize. I'm afraid I must leave you and go open the store for business. Unfortunately, we won't be able to have any meaningful time together until I close up shop. I guess I'll also have to spend the day devising a convincing story for your friend, Miss

Oakley. Surely, she'll come to ask about you when you miss your dinner date."

Sophia stood unmoving, struck dumb with surprise, during Holmes's monologue. Now she yelled, "Dr. Holmes! What is the meaning of this!"

The voice, calm and quiet, came through the grill again. "My dear Sophia, I know this is a surprise, and I do apologize, but you left me no alternative. You can yell and make as much noise as you wish. I assure you the room is more than adequately sound-proofed, and you will disturb no one. I would advise you to conserve your energy, though. Tonight will be busy. I might even close the store early to give us more time together. Until then, ta ta."

Sophia yelled. She screamed. She beat on the walls, the door, the floor. The curses and profanities flying from her mouth embarrassed her even in private. Unease had escalated into terror.

It had never crossed her mind to fear Holmes. Pietzel, yes. But Holmes? What did he plan to do with her? Why did he build this sound-proof room into The Castle? Those questions and a million more caromed around her mind, each scarier than the last. Most chilling of all, though, were the horrible possibilities she conjured in the vacuum of real answers.

As some semblance of sanity returned, she found herself sitting on the floor with her back against the door. Her left shoe lay somewhere out of sight. Her skirt hung in tattered shreds. Her knees and hands swelled with bruises and bled from multiple abrasions. Her breath came in short, gasping bursts, raking through her sore throat as snot ran freely from her nose. Tears streamed down her face, and she didn't feel any urge to wipe them away.

Her labored breath made her wonder if this vault might be more than sound-proof. She blew out the lamp, laid down, trying to remain calm and conserve her oxygen. Gradually, she fell asleep, mentally and physically exhausted.

CHAPTER EIGHT

The pop, pop, popping sound of rain hitting her tent roof, combined with the sound of feet squishing through mud as people walked past her tent, told Annie all she needed to know about the current weather.

She dressed in an oiled leather outfit, complete with a wide-brimmed hat. She packed her ammunition in a special water-proof case and collected her pistol and Marlin. The tent flap opened, and Frank entered. As he let the flap fall closed behind him, Annie set her guns on the bed and embraced her husband. Their lips came together in the kind of comfortable kiss that only twenty years of love filled marriage could produce. The kiss lingered for a pleasant moment, then they held each other.

"How's my lovely wife this morning?"

"A little sad about Sophia leaving tomorrow morning." She snuggled her cheek against his shoulder.

"You've developed quite a strong bond with that young woman."

"I have. I've come to think of her as a little sister. Something I never had. Sure, I had older sisters and a younger brother but, because of the chaotic nature of my childhood, we were never particularly close. Turns out I had a hole in my heart I didn't even notice until Sophia filled it."

Frank caressed her back. "I'm glad. In the past few weeks you've certainly seemed happier than I've seen you in quite a while. Not that you were unhappy before, not by a long shot, but there's a new sort of glow to you."

She dipped her head in agreement, and her eyes welled up a little. "Oh, Frank, I don't want her to return to Ohio. I feel like I've barely begun to know her."

He thought about it, resting his chin on the top of Annie's head. "Maybe after the fair, we can take some time away from the show and go visit her. Meet her family."

She pulled away enough to look up into his face with a huge grin. "I married a genius!"

He smiled at the radiance of her reaction. "It's settled, then. It'll give us some time out of the limelight to be a properly married couple for a while."

With a new plan of action, Annie's spirits picked up. "So, Mr. Genius, tonight is my last dinner with her. I want to do something special. Do you have any ideas?"

"Well, telling her about our intended visit seems pretty special to me, but I think you mean something more immediate and tangible." Annie smiled her special smile at him. As always, his heart melted at the sight of it.

"I suppose you could give her one of your pistols. Don't you have a couple you're not using much anymore?"

"I do." She spun from his grasp, stepped over to her chifforobe, and opened the bottom drawer. "I have a Smith & Wesson Model One, and I think she'd love it."

She removed a bundle and opened the oilcloth to reveal a factory engraved, gold and silver washed, seven shot revolver. It sported a ribbed barrel just over three inches long and had bird's-head rosewood grips. The fine little pistol fired .22 short cartridges and had served her well for several years.

"I'll offer to teach her to shoot when we visit her in Ohio after the fair. Absolutely brilliant, darling!"

Frank grinned and winked. "Glad I could be of help, darlin'. I have to go get ready for the morning show. I'll see you on the field."

"Okay, dear. Thanks."

He gave her a quick peck on the cheek, then left.

The catch released smoothly, and the barrel swiveled up to drop the cylinder into her hand. She took out her kit and gave it a thorough cleaning. It didn't really need it, but she wanted to spend a little more time with it before presenting it to Sophia.

She finished cleaning the handsome revolver, reassembled it, and cocked the hammer. With a swipe of her hand, the cylinder spun smoothly. She held the hammer, allowing it to slide forward as she depressed the trigger. She grabbed a box of ammunition, removed the cylinder once again, and loaded six rounds into it. Replacing the cylinder on its pin, she situated it so, when cocked, it would rotate the cylinder to the empty seventh chamber. This precaution would minimize the chance of an accidental discharge. Sewn inside her vest was a special reinforced pocket, which often concealed one of several small pistols for use during her show. She placed the polished and loaded Smith & Wesson into the pocket, so she would have the gift on her and ready to present to Sophia at dinner.

Footsteps on the porch outside attracted her attention.

"Miss Oakley?" Nick, who did odd jobs for the show, called through the closed tent flap.

"Come in, Nick."

The young man opened the flap. "I got your morning copy of the Tribune." He extended the paper toward her.

"Oh, good. Thank you." Taking it, she reached into her left breast pocket, pulled out one of several nickels, and gave it to him.

"That's too much, Miss Oakley."

"The extra is for your time and energy. Thank you, Nick."

He smiled. "Yes, ma'am. You're very welcome." The coin vanished into his pocket as he turned and walked away.

Annie set the paper on her desk and followed him out of the tent, closing the flap behind her, and strode through the misting rain to begin her day of performances. Her mind filled with thoughts of Sophia's pleased expression when Annie gave her the pistol and told her about the visit after the fair.

When Sophia didn't show up after the show, Annie rushed back to her tent, thinking her friend might have lain down for a nap and lost track of time or something. Upon arriving at her tent, everything appeared as she had left it, with no evidence to indicate Sophia had been there. No one in nearby tents had seen the young woman either.

Maybe she got hung up at work. Annie hopped on her bicycle and headed for the pharmacy.

CHAPTER NINE

Arriving at the pharmacy, Annie found it closed for the day. She pulled the bell rope next to the door and waited. After several minutes, she tried again. She'd nearly given up and had decided to search for other alternatives when Holmes stuck his head out the window and looked down at her.

"Can I help ..." He sounded winded, and his voice trailed off as his face lit with recognition. "Miss Oakley! How good to see you again. Give me a moment and I'll come down to let you in." His head disappeared and a couple of minutes later he opened the door.

"What can I help you with, Miss Oakley?"

"I'm looking for Sophia."

Holmes's expression grew puzzled. "When she left, she said she was going to meet you for dinner."

"She never arrived. What time did she leave?"

Holmes pulled his watch from a pocket and looked at it. Replacing it, he stroked his mustache and considered." The last customer left just after five o'clock.

We locked the door. Sophia brought her bag down and set it by the door, and we began cleaning up.

"I don't know exactly how long we took to clean up and restock the shelves, but I'd estimate roughly thirty minutes. I paid Sophia her final wages, bid her farewell, and she departed. I haven't seen her since."

Annie started to worry. "Did you notice which way she went? Did she catch a streetcar?"

"I would assume so. She only had the one piece of luggage, but I doubt she'd choose to carry it for two miles. I did notice she turned east toward the Midway."

Annie tilted her head. "Will you wait a moment? I have to check something."

Holmes said, "Of course. I've got some custom orders to prepare for tomorrow anyway. I'll start on those while I wait."

"Thank you, Doctor." Annie rushed out the door and turned west. Holmes wondered where she was going. He didn't actually have any custom orders to prepare, but he set up items to appear busy. A few minutes later, he saw Annie pass in front of the windows of the store and out of sight. Eventually, she reentered the pharmacy.

"Dr. Holmes, something strange is going on."

Holmes raised an eyebrow. "Really?"

"Yes. Your neighbors were busy cleaning up for the night, and I spoke to both of them. Neither the jeweler nor Mr. Jameson in the candy shop recalls seeing Sophia at all today. They both know her well. Mr. Jameson was disappointed when she didn't stop in to play a farewell game of 'Nellie Bly' as she'd promised."

Annie thought she saw a hint of worry cross Holmes's face, but it passed quickly, and his eyebrows rose as he had a sudden thought.

"She was very excited about spending the night with you. Maybe her excitement overrode her inclination to visit Mr. Jameson."

Annie tilted her head, thinking. "That makes a certain amount of sense. Except the jeweler didn't see her today either."

Holmes shrugged. "The jeweler is the wrong way from the fair. Why would he expect to have seen her?"

"He was holding a pair of earrings for her. She bought them as a gift for her mother. She wouldn't have left without picking them up, but the jeweler still has them. Also, he swears you closed your shop much earlier than six o'clock." Now Holmes did look worried.

"How odd." He came around the counter and stood close to her. "I don't know what the jeweler is talking about, but I fear something dreadful might have befallen poor Sophia."

Holmes moved with reptilian quickness and lashed out with a hard backhand to the side of Annie's head.

The blow knocked her down and dazed her. Old, hard-won instincts kicked in, and she scooted across the floor. Out of his immediate reach, her hand touched the spot where he had hit her. It came away bloody.

In a light, conversational tone, he said, "I'm sorry it came to this. You're an unwelcome wrinkle in my plans."

Annie's mind reeled, trying to catch up. One realization, though, floated to the top of her confusion as an absolute certainty. "You're a wolf!"

Holmes paused his advance toward her with a confused expression. "Pardon?"

"A wolf. Like my foster parents." She tried to scramble to her feet, but tripped over her skirt. The skirt tore with a hissing sound, leaving a large hole running from mid-thigh to mid-shin, and she fell again, landing on her butt. She scooted farther away from him, her right hand reaching into her vest pocket.

Holmes advanced on her again, "Ah. Why do you call them wolves?"

"They were wicked and mean. They only pretended to be human." This time, Annie made it to her feet, and her hand held the pistol she had intended to give to Sophia. Holmes stood less than five feet from her now, almost within reach. Her leggings showed through the large hole in her skirt.

The click of the hammer sounded loud in the stillness between them.

Holmes froze. "Well, well. You're full of surprises. Put the gun down, and I'll take you upstairs where you can talk to Sophia."

Annie narrowed her eyes. "Sophia's here?"

"Yes. She's upstairs waiting for us to join her." He took a step toward her.

"One more step, Doctor, and I *will* shoot. You know I won't miss."

Holmes stopped with a laugh. "Oh, I have no doubt you would hit precisely where you aimed. I do doubt your ability to kill another human, though."

"You're not human. You're a wolf. I've killed plenty of animals. A wolf like you won't be any different."

"Ah. But you're wrong. You know I'm human. It takes a special kind of person to kill another human in cold blood."

"My blood's anything but cold right now."

Holmes lips turned up in a smile, but his eyes remained cold and flat. The eyes of a hungry snake watching a mouse. "If you make me take the gun from you, I'll be very upset. Things will go much worse for you if I'm upset. You'll have no one to blame but yourself." His voice became hard and commanding. "Put ... the gun ... down. Now." He stepped toward her again.

She stepped back to maintain the space between them. Holmes saw her shoulder slump and noted the resigned expression on her face. His eyes shone with a predatory gleam.

"You're right, Doctor. I can't get my head wrapped around killing you. I'm not even sure I can shoot you."

A genuine smile creased Holmes's face. "There. You see? Now put the gun down."

Annie kept the pistol aimed at him with her right hand while her left reached into the breast pocket of her vest. A puzzled look crossed Holmes's face when he saw the nickel she had pulled from the pocket.

"What do you plan to do with a nickel?"

Now, Annie smiled predatorily. "I can't shoot you, but I can shoot this nickel." She pulled the trigger and he twitched back as the hammer struck on the empty cylinder. She cocked the pistol again as she tossed the nickel toward him. She watched it. It became her world. It was only a nickel, her target. She had shot thousands of targets just like it. She tracked the nickel as it fell toward the ground, leading it just a bit. In some part of her mind, Annie realized the leg of Holmes's pants lay behind the nickel, but before she could fully process the fact, she fired.

The shot hit the nickel. The coin and pellets slammed into Holmes's left thigh, tearing his pant leg and leaving shallow, bloody furrows in his leg. The nickel, propelled by the shot, struck his thigh but didn't penetrate. He collapsed as if punched hard in the leg, clutching the wound and howling.

Annie aimed the pistol at his face. "You're not seriously injured. It's ammunition we use in the show, just small pellets. I reckon it burns like the dickens, though.

"But here's the thing, Doctor. It was easier than I'd anticipated. I think I could beat you to death with this pistol faster than I could shoot you to death with this ammunition. I guarantee, though, if you make any sudden moves you'll never see out of your left eye again."

Holmes's demeanor had changed dramatically. No longer the confident man in charge, now he acted like a wounded animal trying to find a way out of a trap. Annie knew, in some ways, his fear made him more dangerous, but she had dealt with wounded, trapped animals before.

"Now, Doctor, is Sophia really here?"

He glared at her.

She pulled another nickel from her pocket and tossed it into the air, catching it in the palm of her left hand. She flipped the coin and caught it again. The muzzle of her pistol never wavered from his left eye, which followed the trajectory of the spinning coin. "Is Sophia really here?"

Slowly, quietly, he said, "Yes. She ... she's locked in a room upstairs."

"Very good." Flip, catch. "Where's the key?" Flip, catch. Holmes turned his attention away from the coin and focused on the barrel of the pistol. In Holmes's vision, it seemed to grow larger with each passing second.

"It's on a key ring in the right pocket of my trousers."

"Slowly, very slowly, bring the key ring out and slide it across the floor toward me."

Holmes carefully reached into his pocket and removed a ring of keys. With a quick flick of his wrist, the keys flew toward her face while he scrambled backwards and tried to regain his feet. Annie had expected something of the sort and didn't hesitate. She shifted slightly to her right, letting the keys bounce off her left breast and fall to the floor. Her finger stroked the trigger. Pellets raked Holmes's left cheek and shredded a chunk of his left ear. He screamed again and cupped the side of his face with his left hand.

"Last warning, Doctor. The next one blinds you. Is Sophia harmed?"

Holmes's voice quavered. "No, ma'am." He paused, "Well, she hasn't had food or water all day."

The bell over the door chimed. Annie took another step away from Holmes and looked over her shoulder to see the jeweler, Mr. Boeing, peeking in through the open door. He saw the pistol in her hand, but from his vantage point, a display case hid Holmes from him. "Oh, dear. Were those gun shots?"

Annie nodded. "Yes, sir. Please fetch a policeman."

Boeing hesitated for a brief moment, then said, "Of course." He stepped back out.

Annie's full attention returned to Holmes, who had tried to crawl behind the display case, out of her line of fire. "Stop right there, Doctor, or I'll put a round of shot into each of your hands." She doubted her ability to actually follow through on the threat or, in fact, to shoot him in the eye. Shooting him in the ear had made her stomach roil. The thought of really maiming him sickened her. Thoughts of the helplessness a young Annie had faced at the hands of vile foster parents, and what might have happened to Sophia, hardened her resolve. She would do whatever it took, even if her stomach turned inside out and she puked all over herself in the process.

A strong urge to grab the keys and run upstairs to find Sophia welled up inside her, but she knew it would be folly. Waiting for Boeing to return with the police, gun in hand, felt reminiscent of childhood hunting trips, where patience had played an essential role in helping to feed and support her family. Now she waited with the same calm stillness.

Holmes held his injuries, occasionally moaning or whimpering with pain, but he didn't try anything else. Eventually, he found his voice and his composure again. "You know, I owe you my gratitude."

Annie, pulled from her thoughts about hunting, shook her head distractedly. "What?"

"Sophia. I couldn't help myself. I really can't be held accountable for the fickleness of nature, but I'm glad you found me out. I commend your loyalty to your friend and your cunning in discovering my crime, not to mention your quick thinking in overcoming me."

Annie shook her head again, confused. "What are you talking about?"

"Are you familiar with the subject of phrenology?"

"I don't believe so."

"It is the study of a person's nature through the measurement of their skull. This, in turn, indicates the size and shape of their brain." He turned his head to the left and pointed to the area just over his right ear. "See, here. I have a bulge, much larger than average. I have another, matching bulge, on the other side in the same location. This corresponds to the regions of the brain related to destructiveness. In an otherwise healthy individual, these bulges would connote orderliness and a fighting spirit. These traits are common among captains of industry. You would find similar bulges on men like Carnegie and Rockefeller. In fact, I suspect you'd find almost identical formations on your own skull.

"However, when you consider other areas of my skull, such as my underdeveloped region here." He pointed to a region higher on the side of his head. "This region deals with conscientiousness. In short, according to medical science, I was predestined to evil tendencies, and, alas, I am a weak man. I have succumbed to these tendencies. And, I must confess, this is not the first time I have done so."

"That's not science, it's hogwash." Her stomach churned as the implications of his words sank in. "You really need to stop talking now, Doctor. If you don't, I don't think I can be held responsible for my actions. Just now, I'm thinking about shooting you in the throat."

Holmes swallowed hard. He opened his mouth, paused, closed it again. The bell rang again, and Annie turned to see Boeing enter with a police officer in tow. The officer, a young patrolman with clean shaven face and close-cropped sandy hair protruding from the back of his patrol cap, likely had less experience with this sort of thing than Annie had just acquired. The policeman said, "What seems to be the problem?"

Holmes cried, "Thank God you're here, officer! This woman is delusional!" The officer, from where he stood, couldn't see Holmes lying on the floor. Holmes's voice startled him and he jerked so hard his hat nearly fell off.

Annie flipped the nickel, still held in her left hand, into the air. Holmes saw it, and his mouth closed so quickly it made an audible click. He watched as it fell toward his chest. Fear and panic blossomed on his face.

"Officer, my name is Annie Oakley. This man attacked me, so I shot him. Twice. He claims he has a friend of mine, Sophia Russler, locked in a room upstairs."

She turned back to Holmes. "Now tell me where Sophia is or, God help me, I will shoot you in your manhood."

The policeman stepped forward, starting to protest. "Miss Oakley--"

Her face flushed with righteous fury and the fierceness in her eyes brooked no argument. The young officer's protest died a quick, clean death in his throat. She looked back at Holmes. "Where is she?"

Some of Holmes's composure had returned. "You really are a marvelous woman, Miss Oakley. I wish I might have gotten to know you better in our short acquaintance. Now, out of respect for you, I must confess. You're too late."

A muscle in the side of Annie's face jumped. Her voice vibrated with barely controlled emotion, but the pistol in her hand never wavered. "What do you mean?"

He laughed, and she almost shot him again. "I mean that she is dead. You'll find what remains of her in a vat of acid in the basement."

Annie felt like he had hit her again. She lost her balance and stumbled back against one of the shelves, nausea eating at her stomach. Boeing and the policeman looked just as shocked. The officer pulled his own pistol from the holster on his side and told Boeing, "Run to the station house and get Detective Porter. And tell him to bring men to search this building." Boeing turned, fumbled with the door in his nervous rush, and literally took off running toward the police station.

Annie noticed a tremor in the policeman's gun hand. His pistol had probably never left its holster in the line of duty before today. After a moment's consideration, she realized nothing Holmes said could be trusted.

A few controlled breaths helped to calm her mind and clear her head. Now was the time for rational thinking. When more police arrived, they would search the building and find Sophia. If Holmes hadn't already killed her, she would probably remain alive until they found her. Otherwise, it didn't matter. Annie's emotions screamed, "Go find Sophia!" but she clamped down on them and forced them into silence. Leaving the young policeman, so obviously out of his depth, alone with the smart, cunning, and dangerous Holmes could prove catastrophic. Steeling herself, she again pointed the little Smith & Wesson at Holmes.

The bastard smiled at her. Blood trickled from his ragged ear and the pockmarks in his face where the shot had struck it.

"You're really quite fetching when you're mad."

The policeman stepped forward and kicked Holmes in the head. Annie gasped, shocked.

"I'm sorry, miss, but the stuff he was saying ... it got to me. He's crazy as hell and it ... disturbed me. If he kept talking, I think I'd have shot him, and I'm not sure I could have justified it. If he's unconscious ... well, he tried to stand, but lost his balance and hit his head when he fell." The officer shrugged, embarrassed.

They watched Holmes suspiciously for a moment, but he seemed completely unconscious, so they relaxed. Annie set her pistol on the shelf next to her within easy reach. The officer replaced his pistol in its holster, and slumped to the floor, his face ashen.

After a long moment, he looked up and his voice had a slight tremor. "By the way, Miss Oakley, my name is Jenkins. Marvin Jenkins. I saw your show last week. I'm a big fan."

Annie smiled at him and curtsied. The tension eased a bit and, after a while, Jenkins stood again.

About fifteen minutes later, a police wagon pulled up in front of the pharmacy. Ten officers disembarked from the back, lining up on the sidewalk. The driver, wearing rough dungarees over a work shirt, didn't seem to be a policeman. He climbed down, tilted his flat cap back on his head, and started tending to the team of horses.

A large man wearing a rumpled suit and bowler hat climbed down from the seat next to the driver. Coarse black sideburns framed his broad face and ran down his cheeks to connect to a large, wiry mustache. As he entered the pharmacy, his thick fingers shoved an unlit cigar between his plump lips. Jenkins straightened to attention and, as he exited the pharmacy, said, "Detective Porter. Miss Annie Oakley."

Annie started to speak, but Porter held up his hand and shook his head. He looked at Annie. His eyes moved up and down, all business without a trace of lechery. The slow sweep of his eyes seemed to take in more details than most people did in a whole day. Next, he turned and performed the same visual inspection of Holmes and the room.

Holmes had come around after about five minutes, but remained groggy and sullen. He hadn't said anything more while they waited. Now he stared at Porter like a rabbit watching a hawk fly overhead. After a few very long seconds, Porter reached up and removed the cigar from his mouth, tucking it into the breast pocket of his jacket.

"Mr. Boeing was rather unnerved when he told me his story and, I must say, it was rather confusing. Based on what he said, though, and what I see here, I assume this man is Dr. Holmes. There was some sort of disagreement, a struggle, and you shot him. Correct?"

"Yes, sir. Twice. Once in the thigh and once in the ear. I'm firing show rounds, though, so they shoot small groups of shot. Painful, but not likely to be lethal. I had no intention of killing him with either shot. I--" Her words tumbled to a halt as she heard herself babbling.

"I assume you are *the* 'Miss Annie Oakley?' The famous sharpshooter in the Wild West show?"

"I am, sir."

"I must then assume you shot him exactly where you intended to shoot him."

It wasn't a question, but Annie answered anyway. "Yes, sir. Both times."

Porter pointed to the side of Annie's face. "I see blood matted in your hair and on your face. His doing?" He indicated Holmes.

"Yes, sir. He blindsided me and knocked me down. That's what prompted me to shoot him."

Porter glanced at her exposed legging. "He tear your skirt too?"

"No, sir. After he knocked me down, I tripped on the skirt as I regained my feet."

Porter grunted, turned toward the door, and made a waving motion with his hand. One of the officers he'd brought with him entered. "Carney, please take this man outside and chain him in the back of the wagon."

Carney stood just over six feet tall with broad shoulders and thick arms and legs. His nose, broken several times and poorly healed, rested in the center of a flat, craggy face. Carney looked down at Holmes like a surgeon might look at a particularly troublesome tumor he was about to remove from a patient's body.

"Can you stand?" the large man rumbled.

Holmes glared for a moment, and said, "I believe so. I think I can even walk, after a fashion."

Carney shrugged. "Good for you. Get up."

Halfway to his feet, Holmes slumped back to the floor, shaking his head. "A moment, please. Your young officer kicked me rather hard, and I think I might have a concussion."

Porter raised an eyebrow and looked at Annie. Annie just shrugged. She couldn't bring herself to lie outright but would happily let the detective draw his own conclusions. Porter's eyes narrowed for a moment, his brow furrowed, and he gave a tiny shrug. "Carney, help the man up and get him outside."

"Yes, sir." Carney moved over next to Holmes and knelt. He draped Holmes's right arm across his shoulders and rose to his feet. The large officer all but carried Holmes as the two staggered outside. Annie picked up her pistol, released the hammer, and replaced it in her vest pocket.

"Now, Miss Oakley, tell me your story."

"I believe Holmes has harmed a friend of mine, Sophia Russler. First, he said she was locked in a room somewhere. Then he said he'd killed her and dumped her body in a vat of acid in the basement. I don't know which, if either, story is true. Can you have your men start searching?"

Porter pulled the cigar from his pocket and put it into his mouth. It bobbed in small circles as he chewed it in agitation. Being told how to do his job rankled a bit but, after a few moments, he said, "Of course." He motioned to someone outside the door, and Jenkins returned.

"Yes, sir?"

"Organize a search of the building. The entire building from top to bottom. If you can't find a key for a door, break it down."

Annie pointed to the ring of keys still lying on the floor where they had landed. "I'd guess there's a key there for every lock in the building."

Jenkins stepped quickly between Porter and Annie and retrieved the key ring from the floor. As Jenkins exited the pharmacy and gathered men to search, Porter looked around the room, cigar still bobbing in his mouth. Moving toward the back of the room, he motioned for Annie to follow.

He directed Annie to the chair where Holmes had sat while working on his ledgers. Porter took a small notepad and a pencil from his jacket pocket and set them on the counter. The burly detective removed his jacket and laid it next to the tablet. He placed his hat atop the jacket. He unbuttoned his sleeves and rolled them up past his elbows, then picked up the notepad and pencil.

Around the cigar he said, "Start with how you got involved in this and end with us sitting here now. Give me as much detail as you can."

Annie started with meeting Sophia and introducing her to Holmes in the hopes he could offer her lodging at a reasonable price. The cigar danced a jig in Porter's mouth as he listened. Sometimes it hung from the right, sometimes from the left. He occasionally asked a question to clarify something but mostly kept silent except for the mouth noises accompanying his cigar chewing.

As she spoke, part of her mind analyzed the detective in return. She wondered if he smoked cigars at all, or if it was an affectation. Annie suspected he used to smoke but had given it up, maybe for the wife indicated by his wedding band. The act of chewing on the unlit stump probably helped him focus. Muffled bumps and thumps came to her ears, reassuringly, as officers searched the building for Sophia.

Annie, on first seeing Porter, had thought the rumpled suit and apparent nervous habit of chewing the unlit cigar hinted at a tendency toward slovenliness and barely controlled vices. Now, though, she saw a very keen and detail-oriented mind lurking behind the facade. He took few notes and, when he did, he wrote in large printed letters so only a few words fit on each page. Despite the limited notes, Annie suspected he could have recited her story almost verbatim if he chose to do so.

After what felt like an eternity, Annie finished her statement by saying, "Then you arrived, and here we are."

Porter grunted, looked at his notes for a long time, flipping back and forth through the pages. "I believe I have everything I need from you, Miss. You're free to go."

"Go? What about Sophia?"

Porter removed the cigar from his mouth and held it in his right hand, his index finger curled over the top of it. "We have Holmes for assaulting you. I assume you want to press charges."

"Of course! But what about Sophia?"

The detective's hand rose, palm out, in a placating motion. In an apologetic but authoritative voice, he said, "If she's here, we'll find her. If we find her, I'll send an officer straightaway to fetch you. I'm going to be very blunt with you, Miss Oakley. If, God forbid, the suspect was telling the truth about the vat of acid, then we'll likely never really know if we've found her or not. We'll only know we found human remains."

He paused and shook his head. "I guess what I'm clumsily trying to say is, it could take a while. This is a big building. We'll let you know as soon as we have actual news. I hope it'll be good news, but I can't make any promises. From the story you've told me, the suspect is a very disturbed individual. Depraved, even. I'll have an officer escort you back to your lodgings."

Annie shook her head. "I'm not going anywhere."

Porter sighed. "Miss Oakley, I understand your reluctance. I truly do, but there's nothing more you can do here. If you stay, you'll only be in the way. I'm sorry. I really am, and I hope we find your friend alive and unharmed."

Annie filled her lungs, about to argue more. Then she exhaled slowly, her shoulders slumped in resignation. Standing, she nodded. The detective was right.

"Wait outside, Miss Oakley, and I'll get someone to escort you. Jenkins, perhaps?"

"Please, don't trouble yourself. I rode my bicycle here. I'll be fine riding it back."

Just then, the bell at the front door rang, and a tall man strode into the room, followed by a shorter man. Both men walked with brisk purpose. The taller man, especially, radiated a dangerous intensity, setting Porter's instincts on edge.

Annie cried, "Colonel! Frank! What're you doing here?"

Frank rushed forward and scooped Annie up in a hug. He said, "Are—"

Annie silenced him with a kiss.

Cody stepped forward and extended his hand toward Porter. "William F. Cody, sir."

Porter relaxed and shook Cody's hand. "Detective Neil Porter. I need you three to vacate the premises so we can search it properly. Please escort Miss Oakley back to her lodgings, and we will notify you when we have news of Miss Russler."

Cody narrowed his eyes and appraised the detective.

The showman's bearing impressed Porter. He had always thought Cody was nothing more than a showman, and he thought the dime novels were fanciful imaginings based more on hot air than facts. But Cody struck him as a shrewd and seasoned man of action.

After a moment, Cody said, "I understand." He turned and stepped over to stand beside Annie and Frank. Annie stepped out of Frank's embrace and reached up to pull Cody's face toward her. She kissed him on the cheek. As they walked out of the building, Annie asked, "What're you fellas doin' here?"

Cody explained. "I was just sitting down to dinner after going over the books with Nate when a runner arrived. He said he'd been hired by a policeman named Jenkins. Said there was trouble at Holmes's Pharmacy and you were involved. That, of course, was sufficient to rile me. I retrieved Frank. We nearly brought the whole troop, but decided it might be overly dramatic."

Annie laughed as she imagined a veritable army with nearly 500 assorted men and women, including cowboys and military from all over the world, not to mention nearly 100 Indians, riding through the Chicago streets, all armed to the teeth with their various weapons. "I reckon you're right, Colonel. That might have been excessive."

Cody smiled. "Frank and I decided we could handle most any trouble in need of handling, so we saddled up and rode over." Now, they stood about a block east of the pharmacy, next to where Cody and Frank had tethered their horses.

Frank picked up the narrative. "When we arrived, we found this mess of people milling about, and a lot of talk about gunshots. Some folks speculated that you might have been injured, or maybe you had killed someone. No one seemed very sure. There were two policemen standing by the back of the wagon. Cody talked to one of them, and we found out what was really going on. Once we knew you were okay, we hung around and watched through the windows.

"We saw you talking to Porter. You looked well enough, though the patch of dried blood on your face was a mite worrisome. But, we figured if it were serious you wouldn't be sitting there talking like you were. So we waited until it looked like you were finished."

"You guys are wonderful! A girl couldn't ask for better protectors."

Frank grumbled, "I just wish we could have been here sooner. You shouldn't have had to deal with this alone." He took a deep breath. "And, pray tell, exactly what did you have to deal with? Even the policeman we talked to wasn't entirely sure. We've heard gossip about the pharmacist going mad or something similar. He may have hurt a woman who worked for him. Were they talking about Sophia? What happened?"

Annie sighed, not wanting to get into it yet, in such a public place. "Let's meet at Mamma's, and I'll tell you everything over dinner. I think Mamma Aquila will want to hear it too. She's grown fond of Sophia as well."

Frank could read pain in Annie's face, clear as day, and his whole body ached with sympathy for his wife. "Something's happened to Sophia? Where is she?"

Annie voice trembled as she said, "They're searching for her." She broke into tears. The stress of holding herself together for so long had reached a breaking point. Frank took her in his arms and held her. "Cody, can you figure out a way to get Annie's bike back to her tent. She'll ride with me to the restaurant."

Cody said, "I'll handle it. Take your time, and I'll see you when you get to the restaurant."

Annie mounted Frank's horse, an Appaloosa named Black Star. Frank mounted behind her, reached around her, and took the reins. Annie sank back into his chest and felt herself relax for the first time in hours. While Frank guided the horse at a slow walk, Annie closed her eyes.

CHAPTER TEN

Annie and Frank did take their time. They meandered through the streets of Chicago while Frank guided the horse. They talked about trivial things to distract themselves from their worry for Sophia. When they arrived at the restaurant, Cody and Mamma met them outside.

Cody had already filled Mamma in with the broad strokes of the situation as he knew them. Mamma fired off some rapid Italian, and one of the waiters jumped as if goosed. He escorted Cody and Frank back to Annie's regular table.

"You come with Mamma, nipotina. Mamma will take care of you, you'll see." She led Annie through the restaurant, into the kitchen, then up a flight of stairs to an apartment. As they passed through the kitchen, she yelled something in Italian to a woman cutting tomatoes. The woman responded, "Sì, Mamma!"

Mamma had Annie sit in a chair in her private kitchen. "Wait here, nipotina. Mamma will be back soon."

Annie smiled as the petite Italian woman returned with a long skirt. "La mia nipotina can't be seen wearing a tattered skirt. Stand, stand. Mamma had many daughters. Bella, Mamma's third daughter, was about your size." Mamma handed the skirt to Annie and set her sewing kit on the table. "Make yourself decent. Mamma will see what is taking Anita so long with the water." She went out the door and down the stairs to the restaurant's kitchen.

Removing her torn skirt, Annie pulled on the skirt Mamma had given her. It was too long, but not horribly so, and a little loose in the waist. With a few quick stitches, she cinched up the waist and hem so the skirt fit almost as well as her own had. Mamma returned carrying a pale of water and a wooden case. She set the case on the table and the bucket on the floor.

From a cabinet, she retrieved a towel, and dipped it into the water. "Hold still and let Mamma work." As she washed the dried blood from the side of Annie's face, she asked, "Why are you still bloody? Did they not think to let you wash, those policemen?"

Grinning, Annie replied, "No, Mamma. There was a lot going on."

No one had mothered her in a long time, and it felt good. As the cloth scraped over the wound, a small hiss of pain escaped Annie's lips.

"Is bad, but could be worse. You trust Mamma. She was nurse in Italia when she was young. She patched many injured soldiers."

Annie looked at the thin woman in front of her. She tried, and failed, to imagine Mamma as a young woman, or, in fact, as anything other than a restaurateur and cook. After cleaning the wound, Mamma opened the case. As she worked, she spoke in a soothing, nearly hypnotic way. "Mamma kept this kit after war with Austria. Italia helped Prussia beat Austria ... nearly thirty years ago, it was. We won, but at the cost of many good men. That war, though, it is forgotten by most of the world." The woman's hands moved in a professional manner. It took her only a few moments to dress the minor cut and declare Annie ready to face the world again.

The case closed with a click. "Come, nipotina. We will join your handsome men, and you tell Mamma what happened." Annie smiled and followed Mamma back down to join Frank and Cody at the table in the restaurant.

Frank and Cody talked quietly, each with a mug of Pabst Brewery's "Best Select" beer in front of them. The beer, nominated as the best beer at the fair, helped them get a handle on their anger and frustration at the situation. When Mamma and Annie joined them, Frank said, "You look much improved, my dear."

Mamma cleared her throat to get their attention. "Nipotina, tell Mamma what happened."

Annie recounted the tale again. In going over the events with Porter, she'd managed a clinical detachment. This telling, though, held much more emotion. She broke down several times, speechless with crying jags, while her tears stained the shoulder of Frank's jacket as he held her.

Finally, she got through the story. Frank held Annie, tears glistening in his eyes too. Everyone sat silent, absorbing and processing.

After a long, long moment, Cody said in a quiet voice, "I should've shot the scurvy son of a bitch when I saw him in the police wagon."

A chill ran down Annie's spine. She didn't blame him a bit for the sentiment. In fact, part of her also wished he'd shot Holmes, but she was glad he hadn't.

"You would have been arrested, Colonel. He's a vile madman, not worth putting your own neck on the line."

"I reckon you're right, Missy, but it doesn't change how I feel, and I feel like I ought to have shot him."

After dabbing her eyes with the hem of her apron, Mamma extended her hands. "Come. Mamma will lead a prayer for our Sophia." The rest joined hands so they formed a complete circle around the table. They all bowed their heads.

"The ninetieth Psalm is good here." Mamma paused a moment, gathering her thoughts. "Laus Cantici David. Qui habitat in adiutorio Altissimi, in protectione Dei cæli commorabitur." She continued slowly, reverently through the passage, finishing with, "Amen."

The rest of the table echoed, "Amen."

The group sat in silence, still holding hands and heads still bowed, for several minutes, each thinking his or her own thoughts, saying their own private prayers for Sophia. Gradually, hands separated and heads raised.

Finally, Mamma looked around. "Is there more we can do now?"

Everyone exchanged glances. Cody shrugged. "I could still go shoot the bastard. It wouldn't help Sophia, but I'd feel better." They all shared the same sentiment to some degree, and everyone seemed a little more comfortable once he said it aloud.

Annie shrugged. "I'm afraid not. All we can do at this point is wait and pray." She paused. "If something dreadful has happened to Sophia, then we might reconsider shooting Holmes." They all shared a sad grin.

Mamma motioned for a waiter to come to the table. "Tonight you are Mamma's personal guests. Your strange American money is no good here."

The waiter brought Annie a glass of water, refreshed Cody and Frank's beers, then took their orders.

Mamma had meant what she said completely. She wasn't just picking up the bill, the entire staff treated them like family.

CHAPTER ELEVEN

Wednesday, May 24, 1893

Sergeant Burke was not a squeamish man. An Irish immigrant, he'd joined the Union Army at the age of seventeen, following the lead of his friends and older brothers. The bloody battles of the war had laid bare the most horrific aspects of human nature and suffering. He had held friends while they died, seen thousands of dead and dying, and witnessed hundreds of people torn apart by gunfire and explosions. He'd seen, firsthand, the devastation after a mortar round landed amidst troops. He'd held men down while the field surgeon sawed off limbs.

Now, a twenty year veteran of the Chicago police, he'd seen people do some pretty horrible things to each other off the battlefield as well. None of his prior experiences, though, had prepared him for what he encountered in the basement beneath "The Castle."

By the time the officers found the door, locked and half hidden in a dead-end hallway, a noticeable odor emanated from something on the other side. Burke didn't want to wait for someone to find the proper key, so he instructed an officer to bring him a pry bar. Fearing the worst, he sent everyone else away. He forced the wedged end of the pry bar between the door and jam, and pulled hard until a loud pop echoed down the hallway. The latch gave way, and the door creaked open a few inches. A strong, coppery odor wafted through the now open doorway and hit Burke hard. He recognized the smell of blood immediately, and prepared himself for a bad scene.

The white tiled floors and walls reflected light from a dozen bright lamps installed in sconces around the room. The illumination nearly blinded Burke, whose sight had grown accustomed to the darkness of the hallway outside. He shielded his eyes and peered around the room.

His scrutiny stopped on a large water pump with a hose attached in the corner. The hose draped over a hook on the wall next to the pump. As Burke's eyes adjusted to the brightness, he noticed a thick line of black. Congealed blood led from a drain in the middle of the floor toward the back of the room, and Burke's gaze followed it reluctantly. Part of him wanted to avert his eyes, but the stalwart, grizzled veteran of both war and Chicago's rough streets forced himself to continue.

At the end of the trail, a pair of small, pale feet faced him from the end of a surgical table. He inhaled deeply and steadied himself.

In the war, Burke had learned to think of a corpse as just so much meat. Any other approach would have him puking in the corner, and his men couldn't see him in such a state. Plenty of them would lose their dinners before the end of the night, and a sergeant had to be strong for all his men.

He walked across the room, careful not to touch the blood leading from the table to the drain. Beside the table rested a tray of surgical implements. A couple of buckets on the floor by the table contained bits of meat floating in blood, like a cannibalistic soup. The sergeant recognized the scalpel and bone saw from his Army days, but most of the tools on the tray seemed strange and wicked. He looked at the body with as much analytical detachment as he could muster.

A nude female, with a youthful face and long auburn hair draped over her shoulders, lay on the table. Restraints at the wrists and ankles secured her. Two incisions ran diagonally from her shoulders to her breastbone, and another incision started between her breasts and ran down her stomach to her waist. The cuts formed a gruesome "Y." Burke, looking into the cavity of the body, realized the bucket on the floor must contain most of her internal organs. His dinner threatened to come up in spite of his experience and professional detachment.

Her lifeless cornflower-blue eyes stared up at the ceiling. He closed them with practiced reverence.

Why did this scene affect him so profoundly? He had seen things just as bad, maybe worse. After a moment, he realized the horror stemmed from the cold deliberateness of it. As a policeman, he'd dealt with plenty of predators, but some sort of passion had always fueled them. The criminal wanted money or was acting out some sort of power play to prove, at least to himself, his strength, and it was almost always men who committed such acts. Women, in his experience, tended to prefer more subtle and less violent methods of crime.

Here, though, Holmes's motives were beyond Burke's understanding or imagination. He seemed to have killed this young woman simply because he could, and had done it with a clinical detachment the sergeant found utterly unsettling.

He assumed the mess had resulted from an interruption. Otherwise, Holmes would have continued his work to its grisly finale. And, judging by the rest of the building, he would have dealt with the remains and left the room spotless.

Burke walked out of the room. His eyes focused on something ethereal in the distance, something beyond description. His Irish accent unconsciously thick, he called to a couple of the officers nearby. "There's a body in this room. A young one, probably the one we're looking for. We need to get someone down here to identify her. You two watch the door. Don't you go in, and don't you let anyone else go in without my sayin' so."

The two officers took up stations outside the door and, nearly in unison, said, "Yes, Sarge."

Burke walked slowly up the stairs and nodded in greeting at the officers he passed but not really seeing them. He found Detective Porter in the back of the wagon interrogating Holmes.

The detective and the sergeant had known each other a long time and had worked some bad cases together. Porter recognized the look on Burke's face. Without a word, he climbed out to give the sergeant some *quality time* with the prisoner.

Porter called over the two officers guarding the prisoner, and led them down the street about half a block. "Whatever is about to happen, it happened during the excitement before we got Holmes into custody. Understand?"

The two looked at each other, then at Porter. They nodded slowly. One of them said, "What's about to happen, sir?"

Porter shrugged and worked his cigar with his teeth, causing it to bob like a hyperactive chimp at the zoo.

They heard a muffled yell, followed by several thumps. Burke's gravelly voice came to them, yelling something incoherent. Holmes flew from the back door of the rolling jail. The shackles around his ankles were connected to the bench inside, and they brought him up short, causing him to crash head first to the ground, where he lay unmoving for a moment.

Porter began thinking of ways to explain the death of their suspect, but Holmes moaned loudly and rocked his head slowly from side to side. The detective breathed a silent sigh of relief.

Burke slowly climbed down, ignoring the vermin he'd just tossed to the ground, and walked over to Porter and the officers. "Detective, I found a young one in the basement downstairs. She's dead. It's a horrible scene, sir. I believe she's the girl we were looking for, but we'll need a positive identification from someone who knew her."

Porter grimaced. If Burke, a master of stoic understatement, described it as a horrible scene, it must, indeed, be gruesome. "We'll get Cody. Miss Oakley doesn't need to see anything so disturbing." He turned to the officers and pointed to the one on the right. "You. Go to the Wild West show and find Cody. Bring him here immediately."

"Yes, sir."

His finger moved to the other officer, "You. Get the prisoner back into the wagon. Get another officer and the driver. Take the prisoner back to the station. Lock him up. And get a doctor to see to him. Make sure he doesn't die before we can hang the bastard."

"Yes, sir."

CHAPTER TWELVE

It had been a long, stressful night, and Cody had still been on edge when he went to bed. He jerked awake, unsure what had prompted his reaction, but old survival instincts kicked in. He rolled from his bed, hit the floor, and rose quickly to his feet, as he pulled his pistol from its holster, which hung on the chair at his writing desk. He aimed the pistol at the silhouette in the entrance to the tent. A familiar voice said, "Please don't shoot me, sir!"

Cody lowered the hammer on his Colt Navy. In a voice still phlegmy with sleep, he said, "Nick?"

"Yes, sir."

Cody cleared his throat and slid the pistol back into its holster and mumbled, "What the hell do you want, son?" Cody, wearing only his union suit, realized his ass was chilly, and reached back to discover the right button on his drop seat had come undone. He scratched for a moment, closed the flap, and buttoned it.

"Sir, there's a policeman here. Says he needs you to come quick. To identify a body."

"Aw, damn. Give me a few minutes to dress."

"Yes, sir." Nick backed out of the tent.

Cody donned a shirt, buttoned the bottom few buttons, then pulled his pants on, cinched them, and lifted the suspenders over his shoulders. He sat on his bed and pulled on his boots. As he stood, he considered his Colt, still slung over the chair next to the bed.

Speaking to the pistol, he said, "Hell with it. I may still decide to shoot the whoreson if I get the chance." He lifted the gun belt from the chair and strapped it around his waist in its customary, comfortable position. He tied the leg thong around his thigh, grabbed his Stetson from the coat rack, and finished buttoning his shirt as he exited the tent.

The half moon hung low in the western sky as Cody stepped from his tent into the warm night air. The illumination of electric lights at the nearby fairgrounds gave a faint glow to the humid night, which obscured all but the brightest stars overhead. A horse whinnied down by the stables. Folks in nearby tents talked with each other while others snored in their tents.

Nick stood with a policeman, a tall, rangy redhead, in the street outside Cody's tent.

Cody stepped up and extended his hand. "I'm Cody."

The officer shook the extended hand. "Officer O'Malley, sir."

"The boy says you found a body?"

"Yes, sir. We believe it to be Miss Sophia Russler, but we need identification. Detective Porter asked me to retrieve you specifically. Said Miss Oakley shouldn't have to identify her friend."

"I strongly concur. I liked young Sophia, and I will be greatly upset if she's dead, but I have seen plenty of dead folk over the years and, strong as Annie is, she shouldn't have to deal with this when I can do it. Lead on, sir."

O'Malley looked at the pistol on Cody's hip. "Do you really think you need a gun, sir?"

Cody smiled. "Probably not, but I have recently learned there is at least one monster in Chicago. Where there is one, there are likely others, so I reckon I'll wear my pistol."

O'Malley nodded slowly to himself. "Seems reasonable." He led Cody to a small carriage. Cody settled in the back seat, and O'Malley climbed with deft assurance into the driver's seat. He gathered the reins and snapped them, clucking softly. One of the horses tossed its head, then both horses moved forward, pulling them west toward the pharmacy.

CHAPTER THIRTEEN

O'Malley drew back on the reins, bringing the horses to a stop in front of Holmes's pharmacy. The patrol wagon had departed. Cody stepped out of the carriage and, with a purposeful stride, approached the patrolman standing in front of the pharmacy door.

The officer said, "Colonel Cody?"

"The one and only."

The policeman opened the door, and the tall celebrity entered. Standing inside the door, apparently waiting for Cody, stood a young officer whom Cody vaguely remembered from earlier.

"I'm Officer Jenkins."

"Jenkins. You're the fella who sent the runner to fetch me earlier, right?"

Jenkins said, "Yes, sir."

"Thank you, son."

Jenkins shrugged. "Only doing my job, sir. I'm a fan of your show and of Miss Oakley. I had the impression you were a close knit bunch, so I figured you should be informed promptly."

"Well, I appreciate it. We are very close knit. Like family, really.

"You're very welcome, Colonel Cody. If you would, please follow me." As they walked, Jenkins continued, pausing frequently to consider his words. "Detective Porter wanted me to prepare you. The scene is ... disturbing. We're not sure what Holmes was doing, but ... our best guess is that he was ... skinning ... the young woman."

"Skinning her?"

"Yes, sir. Like ... like you might skin a deer. She's opened up in the fashion of an autopsy, but we think she was still alive when Holmes started cutting. There's a lot of blood, and a lot of her guts were removed. The stench in the room is ... daunting."

Cody grunted. Anger pressed against his internal restraints. He followed Jenkins through the pharmacy, into the back room, then down the stairs to the basement. The searching officers had arranged lamps throughout the basement. Jenkins proceeded through the labyrinth of hallways. Cody couldn't keep track of the various turns. At one point, Jenkins muttered, "Shit." and turned around. "Wrong way." He backtracked a bit and, with a sheepish grin toward Cody, turned down one of the side halls they'd passed. Eventually, they arrived at a door guarded by two other officers.

One of the guards rapped on the door, and a gruff voice called from the other side. "What is it?"

The patrolman shouted back. "Jenkins has returned. He's brought Cody."

The door swung open, and Detective Porter stepped out. His ever present cigar hung from the right side of his mouth as he reached out to shake Cody's hand. "Thanks for coming. I've seen worse once or twice, but this is bad. Some of it's downright disturbing, even for me. I reckon you've seen some things in your time too, but I think the warning is still worthwhile."

Cody took a deep breath. "Only way to get it done is to get it started." Porter, harumphed around his cigar, led the way through the door.

Cody stepped through and paused, letting his vision fully adjust to the brighter light. His sharp eyes, trained by years of scouting and tracking, moved slowly around the room, noting every detail. The pump, the drain, the tiles, the trail of blood. Finally, they settled on the surgical table.

The ashen, petite feet facing him from the end of the table made Cody's nerves thrum and his heart race. Porter stood by the table with a uniformed officer and a man in suit pants and an undershirt. Unkempt hair ran in a ring around a balding patch atop his head, and his steel gray eyes watched Cody through thick spectacles.

The uniformed officer possessed the same bearing as all the NCOs Cody had ever met. He radiated dependability and a no-bullshit attitude.

Sizing up the bespectacled man, Cody thought, "He looks like I feel." Cody guessed he, too, had been roused from a deep sleep. The three men, in turn, watched as Cody surveyed the room along with everyone in it. Each of the men, in his own way, was a seasoned veteran, and recognized a kindred spirit in Cody. They gave him time and space to do what he felt he needed to do.

Finally, Cody turned to them and stepped forward. Porter introduced Sergeant Burke and Dr. Cina, the Cook County Medical Examiner. All three men eyed the pistol at Cody's hip for a moment but said nothing. Porter cleared his throat. "Mr. Cody, do you recognize this young woman?"

Cody leaned over and looked at the woman's pleasant, oval face, framed with auburn hair. Analyzed the aquiline nose over full lips. He started to speak, choked a bit, cleared his throat, and lowered his head, pondering how he was going to break the news to Annie. His voice rasped. "Yes. That's Sophia." He raised his eyes and looked at Porter.

Porter swallowed. The conviction in Cody's expression reinforced the detective's previous assessment of the man as more than just a showman with a good publicist. Cody now wore a look very similar to the one Sergeant Burke had worn when he entered the patrol wagon earlier and thrashed Holmes. The face of a righteous man of action who had found evil in his midst. If Holmes had been in the room, Porter was certain Cody would have killed the man without hesitation, then gone back to bed with a smile on his face.

"Thank you, Mr. Cody. I'm very sorry for your loss. Please extend my condolences to Miss Oakley."

After a pause, Cody said, "Promise me this monster will hang."

"I can't promise. The legal system doesn't guarantee justice."

Cody started to say something, but was interrupted by Burke. Aware of Cody's history in the army, Burke reflexively addressed Cody by his rank, "Colonel Cody, sir."

Cody turned to face him.

Burke continued. "I personally promise. I'd rather be hung myself than see this bastard walk." He looked to Porter and Cina for any objections. They offered none.

Satisfied, Cody turned back to Porter and asked, "Do you need anything else from me?"

"No, sir. Once again, I offer my condolences and my thanks for the identification. Officer Jenkins will guide you back up, and make sure you get back to your tent."

The two men stepped onto the porch in front of the pharmacy, and Jenkins offered to bring around a carriage to take Cody back to his tent.

"Don't bother with the carriage, son. I've just swallowed a whole trough of bitter news, and the walk will help me digest it."

With a brief nod, the young patrolman said, "Good night, sir."

Cody stepped into the warm, humid night air and began walking east down 63rd. The odors of lamp oil and horse manure suited his mood. In the distance, the White City's electric lights glowed their faint incandescent hue. He walked, head up, hands clasped and hanging behind his back. How could he break the news to Annie? Ultimately, he decided to say it outright. In her shoes, he'd want to hear it bluntly, and he knew the woman well enough to grasp that, in spite of the pain it caused, she'd appreciate the same courtesy.

With her slender, petite physique, Annie seemed frail, sometimes more like a child than a woman. Over the years, though, he had, time and again, seen the core of steel running through her tiny frame. Her diminutive figure held a reserve of strength comparable to anyone Cody had ever met, man or woman.

Out of respect, he wouldn't sugar coat the news. He wouldn't treat her like she was fragile or soft. He would tell her outright and do whatever he could to help her, and help Frank help her, through the grief. With his mind made up, his stride lengthened and his pace quickened. An old dirge came to mind and he hummed it in low, respectful tones, a personal tribute to Sophia and the friendship she'd shared with his friend Annie.

CHAPTER FOURTEEN

Thursday, May 25, 1893

Annie visited Mamma and told her the terrible news. They cried a long time and, between them, drank a bottle of wine. It was one of the few times in Annie's life she had drunk alcohol, but it felt right to share the pain with Mamma over drinks to numb the worst of the pain.

Annie wrote to people she knew in the Dayton area and, with their help, found Sophia's parents. She sent them a letter that described her friendship with their daughter. The letter informed them of the terrible news and asked if she and Frank could visit after the fair.

Sophia's mother, Sharon, replied. She was, of course, distraught by the news of Sophia's death but glad to hear Sophia, until her death, had such a marvelous experience in Chicago. She said Annie and Frank could visit any time, and she looked forward to meeting them in person. She gave Annie instructions on how to get to the farm.

During the final, chaotic days of the fair, Patrick Eugene Prendergrast murdered Mayor Carter Harrison, Sr. The whole city grieved the death of the popular man. The fair canceled the closing ceremonies in favor of a public memorial service. The Wild West show joined in with a tribute of its own.

For Annie, the memorial for the Mayor reinforced the reality of death and added more weight to the plans Frank and she had made to visit Sophia's family in Ohio. Annie departed the memorial early and went to her tent to grieve in private.

After the memorial, the couple packed up everything but their essentials in the week prior to the close of the fair. On October 31, 1893, they boarded a train, headed for Ohio.

A cloud of dry Ohio dust rose up from the horses' feet and the carriage wheels as Annie and Frank followed the winding dirt path to a large, rambling farmhouse. Frank parked in the shade of an oak tree. A girl, about six years old, ran across the yard, her brown pigtails and yellow flower print dress fluttering in the wind behind her. She ran into the house yelling, "Mamaw! Papaw! There's folks come in a buggy!"

Frank and Annie shared an amused smile, then Frank climbed from the carriage and walked around to help Annie down. A couple came out onto the porch of the house. The middle aged woman wore an apron and a simple blue gingham dress over her stout figure. It was evident where Sophia had inherited her blue eyes and high cheek bones.

The tall, muscular man beside her, Douglas Russler, had a full head of thick white hair over a clean shaven face. A life of hard labor had kept him strong and healthy. From the letters they had exchanged in the months since Sophia's death, Annie felt like she already knew them.

Stepping onto the porch, Annie hugged Sharon while Douglas and Frank shook hands. After a moment, they switched positions and Annie hugged Douglas while Sharon hugged Frank.

Sharon said, "Come in, come in. I'll send the twins out to get your belongings and put them in your room."

Annie said, "You don't have to put us up, ma'am. We're happy to stay at an inn."

"Pshaw, Annie. Y'all are family. Sophia only wrote me a couple of times before ... before she ..." She broke down crying and Annie, tears glistening in her own eyes, put her arm around the older woman's shoulders.

After a moment, Sharon drew in a long draft of air, exhaled slowly, and reined in her emotions before they spiraled out of control. "In the last letter I received from Sophia, she said she thought of you as a sister. That means you're family." She glanced lovingly at Douglas. "My husband is a fair hand at farming, but his true calling is carpentry. The farm keeps us fed and makes a little money in the good years, but Pa's carpentry is what really provides for us. We are a long way from wealthy, but we do have a large, well-built house, and plenty of room."

Annie looked at Frank and he nodded. She turned back to Sharon. "Thank you."

The group entered the house, and the new arrivals met the rest of the family. The little girl who had announced their arrival was Michelle, the daughter of Shawn Russler, the eldest of Douglas and Sharon's children. Shawn and his wife, Emily, had left Michelle at the farm while they went to the hospital in Dayton so Emily could give birth to their second child.

Next, they met the twins, Tim and Sam, who were a few years older than Sophia. They headed outside to collect Annie and Frank's luggage, and the elder Russlers continued the introductions.

Joseph, Sophia's younger brother, and his new wife, Sandra, rounded out the large and energetic family. They had driven their carriage from their house down the road to meet Annie and Frank on this blustery November day.

Douglas took Annie and Frank on a tour of the rambling farmhouse and, ultimately, to the room where Annie and Frank would sleep. A large, canopied bed dominated the small but comfortable room, and their luggage had already been placed in the closet.

Annie turned to Douglas. "Did you make this bed?"

"Yes, ma'am."

"Douglas, you're an artist."

A proud smile lit his face. "I'll leave you folks alone to get settled. I'll go help Ma set the table for dinner. Take your time and join us in the dining room when you're ready."

Annie and Frank unpacked and settled in. Sitting on the bed, Frank put his arm around his wife's shoulders and she snuggled into him. Her shoulders rocked slightly as she cried. He held her close until she leaned back and kissed him on the cheek. "I love you."

He smiled, took her face in his hands, wiped the tears from her cheeks with his thumbs, and kissed her on the forehead. "I love you, too."

After Annie dug into her luggage and retrieved the earrings Sophia had purchased, they joined the Russler clan in the dining room. On the table, large bowls containing mashed potatoes, green beans, and biscuits surrounded a large roast. Frank's mouth flooded with saliva as he held Annie's chair for her and settled himself beside her.

Annie set the small box with the earrings on the table and asked for them to be passed down to Sharon. It took several attempts to speak through her choked throat but, with effort, she explained the provenance of the gift. Sharon cupped the earrings in her hands and brought them to her lips. Her eyes closed, and tears leaked from beneath the lids. No one said anything until the grieving mother opened her eyes and set the earrings beside her on the table.

Douglas extended one hand to Sharon on his right and the other to Tim on his left. Each in turn around the table took the hands of those next to them until they formed a circle with Frank and Sandra reaching across the table from their seats. Douglas lowered his head and everyone else followed suit.

Douglas spoke in a strong, rumbling bass. "Thank you, Lord, for the food we're about to eat. Thank you for bringing our family together like this. Please take care of Shawn and Emily, and see them safely through the birth of their new child. We miss our ..." He paused, choking a bit, then continued, pain obvious in his voice. "We miss our daughter, Sophia, but know she's with you in Heaven and that ... that--in spite of everything--it was your plan, and you needed her with you for some reason beyond our ken. We also thank you for bringing her friends, Annie and Frank, into our lives. Thank you for all your blessings. Please forgive us our petty thoughts, and help us be strong and good people. Amen."

The whole table echoed, "Amen."

Annie looked up. There wasn't a dry eye at the table. Even little Michelle was crying, though Annie didn't think the girl old enough to really grasp the reality of her Aunt Sophia's absence. Annie began to speak. "Mr. and Mrs. Russler ..."

Sharon interrupted. "Enough with the formalities. Call us Douglas and Sharon if you must, but we'd really prefer you call us Ma and Pa. I told you, you're family. My daughter adored you, Annie. Befriending you was a dream beyond her hope, but it came true. She named you sister in one of her letters, and I name you daughter. Here and now." She choked on the last words and turned her face into Douglas's shoulder. He held her. The rest of the table wiped their own eyes and mumbled their agreement. Except for the occasional sniffle, the table sat silent. After several minutes, Michelle appeared at Annie's side. "You're Auntie Sophia's friend, right? Wanna hear a funny story about her?"

Annie laughed, tears streaming down her face. She slid her chair back and lifted Michelle into her lap. "I sure do, little one. Tell your Auntie Annie a story."

Annie and Frank spent three weeks with the Russlers. They met Shawn and Emily when they returned from Dayton with their newborn girl, named Sophia. They even rode into Dayton one day and visited the Wright Cycle Exchange to hear the Wright brothers talk about their crazy ideas for a flying machine.

Annie gave the small revolver, her parting gift for Sophia, to Sharon. Every day, Annie took time to teach Sharon, Emily, and Sandra about shooting. Occasionally, some of the men joined in, but usually it was the women. Annie loved teaching women to shoot. She believed all women should have at least a passing familiarity with firearms.

Frank would sometimes help her teach, but mostly he watched, beaming with pride. She was an incredible teacher, very patient and incredibly good at helping people to understand subtle nuances. Frank had far less patience and, sometimes, couldn't figure out why people had so much trouble learning the simplest things.

Annie and Frank both helped with the chores around the house and farm, and they loved it. By the end of their visit, they truly felt like family. They enjoyed working with the Wild West, and neither planned to give up show business any time soon, but spending some time away from the show had perks, too.

When they left the Russlers, the goodbyes were long, tearful, and heartfelt. Annie and Frank promised to visit as frequently as they could, and if any or all of the Russlers should ever visit the Wild West, or anywhere Annie and Frank were performing, they would be treated as family and welcomed into the troop for as long as they wanted to visit.

As they drove their carriage away from the Russler farm in the coolness of the morning, Annie stretched up to kiss Frank, then settled down close to his warmth. They rode east toward Dayton with the first blush of sun bright in their faces, taking the edge off the chilly air and forming tiny rainbows in the mist of their breath.

AFTERWORD

Story Genesis

I first became aware of Herman Webster Mudgett, aka Dr. H. H. Holmes, and his nefarious activities when I read *Depraved* by Harold Schechter. The idea that Holmes was active during the World's Fair and used his hotel to lure victims into his murderous clutches intrigued me. I had already considered a story involving Buffalo Bill Cody and his show so had done some research along those lines as well. When I realized the Wild West was in Chicago at the same time that Holmes was active, the kernel for this story took root.

I wasn't yet ready to tackle the project, though. I made a lot of excuses, a few of which were even valid reasons, and it wound up sitting on a back burner for years. It kept cropping up, though, like an itch I couldn't quite scratch.

A friend and mentor of mine, Joe R. Lansdale, began posting on Facebook about his personal approach to writing. I found his posts very inspiring and decided to turn my vague interest in writing fiction into a commitment. This story had kicked around my unconsciousness for several years, and it came leaping to the forefront like a hungry hyena scenting a freshly dead zebra.

Amazing Backdrop

As I began my research for this story, I began to realize how amazing the year of 1893 was. Especially in Chicago but, really, the whole world perched on the cusp of some pretty amazing changes. To name a few, some of which even made it into my story:

Thomas Edison completed the world's first movie studio and filmed the first movie close-up. In fact, in 1894, Edison shot a short film of Annie Oakley in action, which you can now find on YouTube.

Edison and General Electric, proponents of direct current electricity, vied with George Westinghouse and Nikola Tesla and their alternating current method for electrifying the Chicago World's Fair. Westinghouse and Tesla won the contract. They also won several other big contracts and, ultimately, won the "War of Currents," and alternating current became the standard in the U.S.

The Wright Brothers opened Wright Cycle Exchange in Dayton, Ohio, and their experiences repairing bicycles proved valuable in their development of a successful airplane. The New York Stock Exchange crashed and caused the Panic of 1893. Mahatma Gandhi performed his first act of civil disobedience. A jury acquitted Lizzie Borden for the murder of her parents. The first Ferris Wheel premiered at the World's Fair. Commodore Perry arrived in Japan. Colorado accepted female suffrage, and much, much more.

Over the next fifty years, the whole world underwent drastic changes. Electricity, telephones, airplanes, and automobiles grew from new and novel ideas and inventions to tried and true technologies around the world. In short, the incredible year of 1893 launched the world into a whirlwind of technological and engineering marvels.

Alternate History

Many of the background elements in this story are historically accurate. The World's Fair, called the *World Columbian Exposition* in recognition of the 400th anniversary of Columbus's voyage, took place in Chicago.

The centerpiece of the fair, the "White City," amazed visitors. This beautiful marvel of architecture and technology, along with many other displays at the fair, heralded some of the amazing changes soon to sweep across the world.

Buffalo Bill's Wild West, denied a place inside the fair, rented property a couple of blocks south of the Midway Plaisance. The show had tens of thousands of spectators and brought in a lot of money, none of which had to be paid to the fair, much to the chagrin of the fair's organizers. This would mark the pinnacle of the Wild West show's success.

I found a picture of Annie Oakley, taken during the World's Fair, seated in a rocking chair outside her tent reading a book near what is now the intersection of Park Shore East and South Blackstone Avenue in Chicago. I used this photo as a guide when I described the interior of Annie's tent.

Sitting Bull, the famous Hunkpapa Lakota holy man and tribal chief, performed as a member of the Wild West show in 1885. He believed the Creator had bestowed Annie's shooting prowess upon her as a supernatural gift.

He and Annie became so close he symbolically adopted her as a daughter and named her, "Little Sure Shot." She proudly used that name throughout the rest of her professional career.

During my research, I was amazed to learn the fair had transported the cabin where Sitting Bull met his untimely demise and placed it on the Midway, no more than three miles from Annie's tent. I found no evidence to suggest Annie did, in fact, visit the cabin, but I believe she would have.

I put a lot of effort into imagining how difficult it must have been for her, and I hope my brief mention of it does the memory of both her and Sitting Bull some measure of justice. Grieving the loss of a loved one is always personal, and each case is unique. The experience, though, is nearly universal.

I took some liberties with the layout of Holmes's "Murder Castle" in my story. In my research, I found conflicting information about its interior.

These conflicting reports confused me at first but, they make sense when taken in context. Only Holmes really knew the details of the layout and, as near as I can tell, a lot of people at the time were so shocked and repulsed they didn't want to investigate very thoroughly.

A mere five years before this story's time line, and six years before authorities actually captured Holmes, news out of London about Jack the Ripper had rocked the world. It horrified many people in America, and they were relieved to think no such monster existed in their land. To find out such a murderer had, indeed, been active for at least a decade was quite a shock. Many Americans refused, at least on a subconscious level, to accept it.

To my knowledge, Annie never met Holmes and didn't personally know any of his victims. They did, however, spend six months in close proximity. Annie's tent sat less than two miles from Holmes's pharmacy.

This fact led me to ask "what if," which is the lynchpin of alternate history. Through my research, I learned a lot about Cody and Annie and gained a lot of respect for both of them. In my mind, they evolved from historical icons into actual people, and the act of visualizing them, developing them as characters, deepened this respect even more.

Years after writing this story, I visited a museum in Greenville, Ohio. Annie grew up in Darke County, near Greenville, and the museum has a room devoted to her. Visiting that room, walking among Annie's possessions, and reading the plaques with facts about her life felt like spending time with an old friend.

I hope the real Cody and Annie, if they could read this story, would deem my portrayal respectful and consider the story plausible within the context of its "what if."

Most importantly, though, I hope you, the reader, enjoyed this walk with me through my version of 1893 Chicago.

ABOUT THE AUTHOR

I currently live in an RV and travel the nation to teach *AGPS*, which is my martial arts system. As far as I know, I am the one and only *Wandering Guru.*

As I write this, I'm sitting in my room in a hostel in Cuenca, Ecuador. My wife and I plan to move here after she retires.

Made in the USA
Columbia, SC
04 September 2017